P9-CQH-207

ORFEIA

By Joanne M. Harris from Gollancz

ORFEIA

Joanne M. Harris

Illustrated by Bonnie Helen Hawkins

GOLLANCZ

LONDON

First published in Great Britain in 2020 by Gollancz
an imprint of The Orion Publishing Group Ltd
Carmelite House, 50 Victoria Embankment
London EC4Y 0DZ

An Hachette UK Company

1 3 5 7 9 10 8 6 4 2

A CIP catalogue record for this book is
available from the British Library.

ISBN (Hardback) 978 1 473 22995 2
ISBN (eBook) 978 1 473 22997 6

Printed in Great Britain by Clays Ltd, Elcograph S.p.A

MIX
Paper from
responsible sources
FSC® C104740

www.joanne-harris.co.uk
www.gollancz.co.uk

Prologue

≈

Der lived a king inta da aste,
Scowan ürla grün
Der lived a lady in da wast,
Whar giorten han grün oarlac

Child Ballad no. 19: *King Orfeo*

One

They say the madcap Queen of May once fell in love with a man of the Folk, and followed him to his World, forsaking her life and her memory. All of Faërie grieved for her, and longed for the day when she might return, but the Queen had forgotten her kingdom, her glamours, her kindred and even her name, so that she could never look back, or recognize her people. Only sometimes, in her dreams, did she catch a glimpse of what she had lost, and heard the music of days gone by, and awoke with tears on her pillow. And yet she was happy with her man and the daughter they had together.

But the lives of the Folk are as brief and as bright as skeins of summer lightning, and soon the man grew old and died, and the Queen and her daughter were left alone. Even in her grief, the Queen's daughter was all she needed. But with the death of her father, the child had grown fearful and melancholy. Once as bright as the sun on the sea, she grew ever more listless and forlorn. Her hair, which had been long and fair, grew as fine as spider silk. And in her dreams, she saw a man with eyes the shade of a moth's wing: a man who never spoke or smiled, and walking, cast no shadow.

Almost every fairy tale begins with the death of the parents. But the death of a child changes everything. The death of a child means no journey; no coming-of-age; no adventures; no happy-ever-after. All that remains of the tale is grief. Grief, the wingless bird in its cage, singing and singing and singing.

But a song can climb higher, live longer, see more than any bird that ever flew. A song can pass from mouth to mouth, changing with the seasons. And a song can pass between the Worlds, even to the Kingdom of Death, where the Hallowe'en King on his bone-white throne watches the Worlds through his all-seeing eye, and contemplates the honeycomb.

This is the story of such a song. A song born of a mother's grief, given wings by a mother's love. A song of memory, and loss, and of the magic of every-day things. A song of rebirth, and rejoicing, and a love that lasts for ever. The song of a journey to Death and beyond.

And it starts with the death of a daughter.

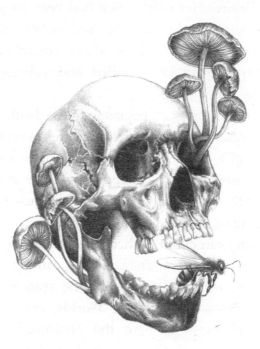

Step on a Crack

≈

My plaid awa, my plaid awa,
And ore the hill and far awa,
And far awa to Norrowa,
My plaid shall not be blown awa.

Child Ballad no. 2:
The Elphin Knight

One

When Daisy Orr was six, she began to avoid the cracks in the pavement. It started as an unusual attentiveness to paving slabs, a reluctance to walk over cobblestones, and evolved into a complex series of skips and jumps and diversions, designed to carry her safely across the many pavements of London.

Children are ritualistic. Their lives are filled with ancient lore. *Step on a crack, break your mother's back* acquires a grim significance for a child who has just lost her father. But six is a resilient age. While her mother struggled with grief, Daisy was coming to terms with death in a way she could control. The pavement game was Daisy's way of making sense of the irrational.

This, at least, was what her mother believed. Later, she came to reassess her reading of the pavement

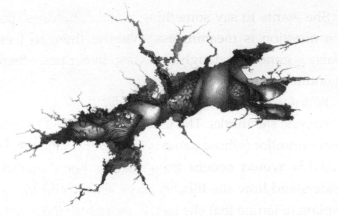

game. But by then it was too late and she herself had slipped through a crack, into a world without Daisy.

There should be a word, Fay Orr tells herself, for a woman who loses a child. A woman who loses a husband can at least put a name to her loss. She is a widow. Her grief has a name. That name gives her a narrative. But this is a different kind of grief. She is a woman who has lost a child. She was a mother. Now she is not. Now she does not know who she is. Now she is adrift, alone. Nameless, she casts no shadow.

Who am I? she asks herself. *What am I doing in this world?* It all seems very wrong, and there is no one here to tell her what to do. She has tried counselling. It doesn't work. Words and affirmations have no meaning any more.

How are you feeling this morning, Fay?

She wants to say something. Really she does. But the question is meaningless. What is there to feel? Daisy is gone. Her daughter is gone. In her place there is nothing.

Why don't we look at your diary, Fay?

Ah yes, she thinks. The diary. It's supposed to help her counsellor (whose name is Janine, and who thinks that Fay would benefit from sharing her thoughts) understand how she fills her days. Fay would like to explain to Janine that she has no thoughts. She is only a mechanism, going through the meaningless rituals over and over every day.

You're keeping fit. That's good, Fay.

Janine is a great believer in the healing properties of exercise. As if tighter calves or more defined abdominals might help her reach an epiphany. Fay knows better. The running has become a compulsion. King's Cross to Trafalgar Square without stepping on a single crack. Euston Road to Regent's Park without thinking of Daisy. The thing is, Daisy is everywhere. Daisy at three; Daisy at six; Daisy dead at twenty-one, stolen away by the Shadowless Man. Children look to their parents to tell them monsters don't exist. But what if they do? Fay asks herself. What if the monsters were here all along, but only Daisy saw them?

This is excellent progress, Fay. Any more dreams?

She shakes her head. There are no dreams she wants to share. Dreams are how this all began. Besides, there's only one dream that counts. She has it almost every night. She dreams she could have saved Daisy, somehow. That she could have known what was happening.

It's not your fault, Janine repeats. *There's nothing else you could have done. Daisy was suffering from a neurological disorder. She was off her medication. There was no way you could have known.*

But that isn't true. There have always been ways. Secret ways to see the world, through dreams and charms and mysteries. Daisy believed in the power of dreams, though Fay dismissed her fantasies.

And now, every night, Fay dreams that she arrived in time to save her. That instead of those twenty-four hours she spent in ignorance – watching TV, going to the gym, sitting in the garden and listening to the sound of the birds – she had somehow instinctively known. That instead of reading an email, she had guessed by osmosis. And now there is no way to banish the thought: *Daisy fell through the pavement cracks. I wasn't there to save her.*

And so she runs. She runs through the pain. When she can no longer run, she walks until she can run again. The pain is like a dark cloud that shows no sign of lifting. People are no more than shadows here. Only the cracks in the pavement are real. Sometimes Fay wonders whether it is she who has slipped through the worlds, somehow. She feels she has become as flat and blank as a piece of paper; trapped between the pages of a continuous narrative, in which Daisy's death replays over and over, like a fragment of dialogue that no longer has any meaning.

Once, she might have turned to music to console herself. Music has been at the heart of Fay's life; music, singing and the stage. It was her husband's life as well – he was a concert pianist. But Allan Orr is as dead as an empty stage in the moonlight, and Daisy is a silent ghost that music cannot exorcize.

And so Fay runs – always at night – along the towpath from King's Cross: or along Euston Road into the West End, Shaftesbury Avenue, Leicester Square, Piccadilly Circus. She likes to run in the small hours, when there is no one else around but the homeless people. Barely visible by day, at night, when the theatres and pubs are closed, when the last Tube home has gone, they come out into the light of the bright shop windows. And there they sit drinking and smoking on the tiled floors by the department stores, wrapped in blankets and bedclothes like children up late on Christmas Eve. Fay feels no urge to speak to them, and yet she feels a kinship. They, too, have slipped through the cracks. They, too, cast no shadow.

She has no destination in mind. She has no sense of time passing. She feels no sense of achievement at having run so far, so fast. The best she can possibly hope for, she knows, is the oblivion of exhaustion. And so she runs with her backpack through the broad, bare London streets in her running shoes that do not match her leggings or her T-shirt: runs past the displays of jewellery, of toys and household objects; feet pounding the pavement slabs; running, as if from a predator.

And yet, there is something different tonight. Something in the air, perhaps. She remembers that it is Michaelmas, the end of the harvest season. Even the city knows it somehow, in its ancient, forest heart. The shadows will lengthen after this: the city will swing into darkness. The leaves are already falling fast; there is a change in the sound of the wind. And tonight, the sky is cold and clear, with the full moon standing sentinel.

There are no stars in London. The city is too bright for their pure, cold light to compete. But the moon is full for the second time this month, and larger than she remembers. *They call that a blue moon*, she tells herself. She does not recall how she knows this. The blue moon rises above Shaftesbury Avenue, luminous as a jellyfish. She moves to get a better view, and as she does, her foot catches on something. Only on looking down does she realize that the paving stone on which she is standing is cracked right down the middle. For a moment she is still, looking down at the paving stone. It must be a trick of the moonlight, but in that moment it looks as if the stone is illuminated *from below*; as if there is a crack in the world, through which a light is shining.

She does not know for how long she stands, pinned by that mysterious light. But it is in that time – seconds, or hours, she does not know – that Fay slips through the crack in the Worlds, into another story.

TWO

She must have blanked out for a moment, she thought. Wasn't the blue harvest moon supposed to have magical properties? Fay did not believe in such things. But there *was* something magical here. She felt it like an ache in her teeth; her mouth was filled with sweetness.

She looked down, but the light at her feet had been replaced by a shadow so dark that she could not see the ground. The lights from the theatres and billboards were gone, overlaid with darkness. And there was a scent, too; a distant scent of woodsmoke. Woodsmoke, on Shaftesbury Avenue? Looking towards Piccadilly, she saw that *all* the streetlights were out. On Regent Street; on Coventry Street; around the Shaftesbury fountain. The Coca-Cola sign was dead; and over Piccadilly Circus there was nothing but moonlight...

A power cut, she told herself. Or maybe a cost-cutting measure. At this time of night, who would even know? And yet it made her uneasy to see the familiar landmarks darkened. It made her imagine all kinds of things hiding in the shadows. She made her way slowly down the street towards Piccadilly Circus. The scent of woodsmoke was stronger now, mingled with something else; a scent of cedar and spices and sandalwood. Looking up, there was another surprise: she could finally see the stars.

Three

Her eyes took a minute or two to adjust, but the moonlight was surprisingly bright; bright enough to cast shadows, and the stars formed an astonishing bridge of light, spanning the city skyline. There was no light at all from the streets: no shops, no billboards; no street lamps. Even Centre Point was dark. The power cut must be city-wide. Except for a dim and flickering glow around the entrance to the Tube, a glow that looked like firelight.

Slowly, Fay moved closer. The scent of smoke was stronger still, making her think of Bonfire Night, and fallen leaves, and fireworks. As she reached the statue of Eros, she saw a group of people huddled around a burning container, which might have been a galvanized pail. They looked like homeless people; their faces bright with reflected fire. Fay counted five; a pale man with long hair; a teenage girl in a wheelchair; a woman in a long coat and two others of ambiguous gender, one slender and purple-haired, the other heavily tattooed, and wearing a patch over one eye. They turned towards her as she approached: even in that moment of calm, they looked ready for battle or flight. They could have been storybook travellers, she thought, sitting around a campfire; pirates, on the deck of a ship; adventurers in a hostile land.

She raised a hand in greeting. 'What happened to the lights?' she said.

The pale man, who was closest to her, gave her an appraising look. His eyes were dark and pinned with gold, like spinners in the firelight. Looking at the Tube entrance, Fay saw that the gate was open, and there was a haphazard pile of tents all the way down the stairs and beyond.

Daisy had a tent, she thought: midnight-blue, and embroidered with stars. She used to sleep there in summertime, on a bed of cushions, surrounded by stuffed animals – cats and bears and elephants; tigers and dogs and unicorns. The animals were supposed to stop the Shadowless Man from getting in. But the Shadowless Man always got in. However many mirrors they placed, or animal guardians, or strings of lights. The Shadowless Man would always come, with his sackful of dreams. Fay wondered if she was dreaming now. And she realized, with a little jolt, that for the past ten minutes or so, she had not thought of Daisy at all.

'You're limping,' said the pale man. 'Sit down.' He indicated a fishing chair set up by the side of the fire pail. His voice was gently accented, but she could not tell the region. Now Fay could see him more clearly, she saw that his dark hair had been shaved along one side and left to grow long on the other. A sickle of diamond studs in one ear gave him a corona of fire.

'What you run for, anyway?' said the girl in the wheelchair. Her voice, too, was accented – more so than her companion's – and her face was broad and brown, her eyes as bright as a bird's. 'You a fitness freak, or what?'

Fay shook her head.

'So what *do* you do?'

'I used to sing.' It was true, though now it seemed like a story to her, a montage from another life. She remembered singing Daisy to sleep with songs from *Assassins* and *Company:* remembered how Daisy slept on the couch in the dressing room at the Palace, or watched her from the wings at the Queen's, her eyes drowned in reflected lights.

'You famous, then?' said the girl. 'Done anything I might've heard of?'

Fay shrugged. That's what they always ask. They always imagine it's glamorous. A few stage roles in the West End, back when Allan was alive. Some concert tours, with songs from the shows. There was even a CD or two. Then mostly ensembles, and character parts, then panto and adverts, and audiobooks. Then nothing. It had been years since she sang. She wondered if she still knew how; what would happen if she tried.

'I quit. I lost my voice,' she said.

'Too bad,' said the girl in the wheelchair. 'Where did it go? Down the back of the sofa, I'll bet, or over the sea to Norroway.'

Did she really say that? thought Fay. *Or did I just imagine it?* Since Daisy died she has been finding it hard to separate dream and reality. Dreams are supposed to be unreal, filled with fantastic details. But now it is *reality* that seems like make-believe to Fay; a world turned on its head, in which Daisy no longer has a part.

'Quiet, Cobweb,' said the man. 'Mind your manners. We have a guest.' Once more addressing Fay, he said: 'Don't mind her. She means no harm. Sit with us awhile, and rest. These are my friends. Cobweb, you met. Here's Mabs, and over there are Moth and Peronelle.' He indicated the other two; Moth with the tattoos and the eyepatch; Peronelle with the purple hair. He held out his hand. 'I'm Alberon.'

Fay gave her name, and allowed the man to lead her to the fishing chair. His fingers were strong and slender, adorned with many silver rings. And there was a scent that clung to him; something like woodsmoke and spices, a woodland scent somehow, she thought – a world away from Piccadilly Circus. Fay sat down, feeling suddenly tired and dazed. Someone – the woman he called Mabs – handed her a plastic cup of some kind of spirit, hot and harsh, but comforting as it settled. The taste was strangely smoky, but sweet, and it went to Fay's head almost at once. Mabs poured another shot.

'Drink up. Winter's in the wings.'

Fay sipped a little more. She wondered how Alberon and his friends would manage once the weather turned. She had heard of rough sleepers finding their way underneath the city, into the disused Tube stations and under ventilation grates. Was this what they had done? How had they managed to open the gates that led to the Tube station, anyway?

Mabs reached into the fire pail and lit a skinny cigarette. The scent was both familiar and strange, the smoke as strong as incense. She cupped her hands around it, sending tendrils of smoke around her head.

In the light of the fire it was hard to tell her age or ethnicity. Her face was small and sharp-featured, and her long hair might have been white or blonde, arresting against her dark skin. She was wearing a long velvet coat that might have been blue, or purple, or brown; opulent in the firelight, though Fay could see it was ragged and worn. Behind her Moth and Cobweb shared one of those tiny cigarettes, its scent both unidentifiable and tantalizingly familiar.

'Here. Try one,' said Alberon, handing his cigarette to Fay.

She started to refuse – she had not smoked for twenty-two years – and yet the contact was welcome. She took a drag of the cigarette – it didn't taste of tobacco at all, but of something like oak moss, and acorn wine, and honey, and fresh popcorn. And it gave her an immediate buzz – a warm and sleepy feeling that seemed to wrap around her like a coat lined with thistledown.

Alberon smiled. 'Feel better?'

Fay nodded, and in that moment, she realized she actually *did*: that the iron-grey mist that had swallowed her life had somehow gently lifted. For how long, she could not say, but for now the sensation was new and wildly exhilarating. She glanced up at the moon, and it looked so large that it might have been a hot-air balloon landing over Eros.

'That isn't really Eros, you know,' she said, through a mouthful of sweet-scented smoke. 'That's his twin brother, Anteros, the god of selfless love. They look just the same, except that Eros's wings are like a bird's, and Anteros's like a butterfly.'

Alberon smiled again. 'Is that so?' Fay was surprised she had spoken aloud. The words danced around her like butterflies on tiny little golden wings. *Butterfly is a golden word*, she thought. *It smells of honeycomb.*

'Don't be alarmed,' said Alberon. 'You're not used to madcap. It won't do you any harm, but it might make you see things differently.'

Fay looked at the cigarette in her hand. *Madcap?* she thought. *What on earth's that?* A cloud of golden butterflies rose from the fire in the galvanized pail and crackled across the face of the moon like a spray of fireworks. A scent came with them; a rich, sweet scent like roses steeped in honey. A little cascade of tumbling notes unrolled and dispersed into the air. Fay looked around and realized that Peronelle was singing.

> *The elphin knight sits on yon hill,*
> *Bay, bay, bay, lily, bay*
> *He blows his horn both loud and shrill.*
> *The wind hath blown my plaid away.*

The song was unfamiliar, the words so heavily accented that she struggled to find their meaning, and yet something in Fay responded to them in a deep and instinctive way. The little notes blew like dandelion seeds, tumbling into the golden air, and to her surprise she found herself laughing aloud in simple joy.

'Every sage grows merry in time,' said Alberon, still smiling. 'Madcap is as madcap does, my Lady, Queen Orfeia.'

'*What did you call me?*' Fay tried to say, but the madcap, or whatever it was, was really starting to take effect. She could feel the smoke in her mouth turning into musical notes; brittle little quavers and crystalline semiquavers taking flight like fireflies.

'Sing with us,' said Alberon. 'Sing with us, and all will be well.'

It would have felt so good to sing again, even for such an audience – and yet she found she could not. Even under the madcap's spell, something kept her silent: the notes that fluttered on her lips were as soundless as falling snow. Peronelle continued to sing: a tune Fay almost felt she knew:

> *Queen Orfeia crossed the bay,*
> *Bay, bay, lily, bay*

Cross'd the sea to Norroway
The wind hath blown my plaid away.

The others joined in: she could see their words;
Alberon's dark and heavy as ink; Mabs' like a ladder
of silver thread; the other three, little dabs of light
against the coral darkness. But even now, when she
could see the notes and feel the harmonies, Fay still
could not find her voice. And so instead she danced;
first alone and then, when Alberon reached out, within
the circle of his arms.

'I would so love to hear you sing,' he said in his low
and pleasant voice. 'Music and madness are lovers,
my Queen. And memory – who needs her?'

Fay smiled. 'Memory is a mother,' she said. 'I could
no more give up my memories than I could lose my
shadow.'

The madcap had reached a kind of multisensory
climax. Music blended with colour and light; scent
and taste with movement. Mabs was dancing with
the smoke, the skirts of her long coat carding the air.
The moonlight was singing in shades of marshmallow
and violet; the motes from the fire were like little bells.
Alberon's hand was at her waist, the other was cool
at the nape of her neck. And they danced like lovers
in the smoke, which smelt of rose and sandalwood, of

cardamom and clove, until at last the music stopped, and the song came to an end.

Peronelle started to clap – not entirely approvingly, Fay thought. 'Brava, Queen Orfeia!'

That name again. 'I'm Fay,' she said.

'Of course you are,' sang Peronelle. 'Fay and fey as Fae can be.'

> *Madcap as the Queen of May;*
> *Heartless as the harvest moon.*
> *Thankless as the thistle-tree,*
> *The wind has blown my plaid away.*

'What does that even mean?' Fay tried to stand, and found her legs unreliable. She threw out her hand to steady herself, and just then she saw a light shine out from under a broken paving stone; a yellow strip of brightness like the light from under a door. No sooner had she noticed it, it went out. She imagined people behind the door, watching, hiding; breathing in the dark.

She pulled away from Alberon's grasp and turned to Peronelle. 'What was that?'

Peronelle laughed. 'That's madcap for you.'

'There was light under the pavement. A *light*.' As Fay's anxiety mounted, she sensed the madcap responding. The feeling of delirium was gone; now her skin was all prickles and thorns. She felt as if she was on the verge of awakening from an ominous dream; as if all the colours in the world were draining into the ground, one by one. Peronelle went on singing, in a voice that was sweet and mocking:

> *Merry as the marigold*
> *Careless as the columbine*
> *Faithless as the foxglove fair*
> *My lady, Queen Orfeia.*

Alberon said: 'That's quite enough.' He put his hand on Fay's shoulder. 'Don't mind Peronelle, my Queen. It's the madcap talking.'

He turned towards Peronelle and made a gesture of dismissal. 'Leave us. Let's have no more talk. Queen Orfeia and I have private business to discuss.'

Peronelle pulled a spiteful face. For a second Fay saw their outline shimmer, as if caught in a heat-haze. Then they dispersed into a cloud of tiny dancing butterflies that rose into the bonfire smoke and vanished in the moonlight. The butterflies were luminous, and all the same shade of purple as Peronelle's hair. Alberon made the same gesture of dismissal to Cobweb and Moth, and both of them vanished in the same way,

Cobweb into an emerald cloud, Moth into a silvery one. The butterflies rose out of sight, briefly covering the moon, then they were gone, and only he and Mabs remained beside the dying fire.

Fay looked down the street, and saw the bar of light had reappeared. The warm glow beneath the stones was back: cheery and enticing, like the light from around a secret door where a riotous party was going on. She stood up, feeling less disoriented. The last of the madcap had given her a reckless kind of determination, and though Alberon's hand tightened on her arm, she pulled away from him, towards the glowing paving stone.

'I wouldn't,' said Alberon gently. 'You're safe here, for the moment. But step off the path again and there's no knowing where in the Worlds you'll end up.'

But Fay was already crossing the road towards the bright crack in the pavement. The darkened shop windows reflected the moon in silent silver panels. She half-expected the light to go out again as she reached it, but this time it stayed, shining out between the slabs of heavy London stone.

Fay knelt to look more closely, putting her face to the crack in the ground. It was no more than half an inch wide, but the light was so brilliant that she had trouble focusing. And yet, as her eyes adjusted, a scene emerged, far away below her, but still as clear and bright as a child's snow-globe. She saw a clearing in a wood, a clearing surrounded by hawthorn trees. Their blossom was as white as snow, and fluttered like confetti. Within the clearing itself, the ground was covered with bluebells – their sleepy scent reached her faintly through the crack in the pavement. And there, asleep in the bluebells, was a girl all dressed in white, under a blanket of wild rose—

For a moment there was no air in the air she was breathing. Her throat was tight; her mouth was numb; her heart was a burning ball of wire...

'*Daisy?*' she said.

The girl slept on. Far under the streets of London, she slept, cocooned in the scent of bluebells.

Fay tried to prise up the paving stone with the tips of her fingers, but the slab was unmoveable. She felt a fingernail tear to the quick; but the pain came to her from a distance, like something that happened to someone else, far away and long ago. From a distance, she could hear the sound of voices behind her: Alberon and Mabs were having an argument.

'Let her be, for pity's sake,' said Mabs. 'What good can you do her now?'

'I will not lose her,' said Alberon. 'Not after all we've been through. Queen Orfeia...' He raised his voice. 'Your Daisy cannot hear you. She sleeps in the hall of the Hallowe'en King, and nothing you do here can wake her.'

But Fay was only aware of him as part of a background of white noise. Once more she called her

31

daughter's name, ringing it off the concrete and glass and stone of Piccadilly. The madcap must still have been working, because her call took shape in the air, rocketing into the sky and coming down in a shower of stars.

Through the crack in the pavement, the sleeping girl turned over and sighed.

Mabs said: 'It's pointless. You've lost her.'

Fay shouted, 'Daisy! It's me! I'm here!' and hammered her fists against the stone, but only managed to bruise her hands.

Below her, the sleeping girl slept on.

Alberon sighed and said: 'We'll find her again in London Beyond. That is, if she gets that far.'

And at that he and Mabs disappeared silently into the smoke, he into a cloud of black butterflies, she into a cloud of silver ones, and if Fay had been watching them, she might have noticed that as they stood together in the moonlight, neither the man nor the woman had cast even the smallest shadow.

As it was, she barely saw them go. Instead she screamed and wept and clawed at the luminous crack in the ground that shone with such a fugitive gleam. But just as her fingers could not lift the stone, her voice seemed to bounce off the pavement, like fireworks hitting the ground. And then the light went out as suddenly as it had appeared, and Fay was left in darkness, alone, under an emptiness of stars.

Four

She must have slept, she told herself. How that could be, she did not know. Perhaps it was the madcap. In any case, when she awoke it was light, and the sky was blue, and she was wrapped in a blanket, with her backpack as a pillow, at the bottom of the steps under the statue of Anteros.

For a moment she was disoriented. Her muscles ached and her mouth was dry. She looked at her Fitbit. Seven-fifteen. She had spent the whole night here. It took her a moment to realize that there was no one else around. This went beyond the unusual, she thought, into the realms of fantasy. A deserted Piccadilly at night was already strange enough, but by seven in the morning, the streets should have been filled with commuters, and retail workers, and street-sweepers,

and taxicabs, and delivery vans, and garbage men, and junkies, and joggers, and tourists. All the same, the streets were bare, both of vehicles and pedestrians. There were no people leaving the Tube; no rough sleepers by the entrance.

Something must have gone wrong, she thought. Maybe there had been a crime. Perhaps the square had been cordoned off by the police, and somehow she had slept through it. She stood up, automatically rolling up the blanket. It was blue, with silver stars, and some part of her mind seemed to recognize it, although she had no memory of bringing it with her on her run. But it was small, and she managed to fit it into her backpack along with the few things she always carried on her night-time runs: a bottle of water; some cereal bars; a purse containing emergency cash; a hoodie in case the night turned cold; her phone; a small first-aid kit; her keys on a key ring shaped like a tiny notebook. She looked down Shaftesbury Avenue, then across the square towards Regent Street. There was no one to be seen, not even where Alberon and his friends had had their fire at the mouth of the Tube. She walked to the spot where the fire-pail had been, but there was nothing left but a little pile of ash and a circle scorched against the stone.

The fire was real, said Fay to herself. *That means*

it wasn't all a dream. The idea that she might have invented Alberon and his friends – perhaps as part of some fugue state – had occurred to her. She looked around for more traces. But the Tube entrance was closed again; the ornamental gates bolted shut, and, looking down into the dark, Fay thought she could see some kind of creeper – bindweed, or bramble, or Russian vine – growing across the stairway. And there was something else too, deep in the tangle of creeper – Cobweb's discarded wheelchair, at the foot of the stairwell.

This must *be a dream*, she told herself. *I dreamed, and am still sleeping.* And yet she could feel the strap of her backpack against her shoulder; the ache of her sore calves; the dryness at the back of her throat. She could still smell woodsmoke on her clothes, and the residual scent of madcap. What had it been? Some new strain of marijuana? Whatever it was, she felt sober now. She found her water bottle in the pocket of her backpack and drank. The water was cool against her throat, and she felt a little better.

It must have been a fugue state, she thought. That would explain the things she had seen, and her mind had merely attempted to fit them into her reality. But now she felt completely awake, completely sober, and yet this was still not the London she knew. She wanted

to go home, but the Tube was closed on both sides of the square. So she started to walk along Piccadilly, conscious of the sound of her feet on the silent pavement, and as she did she remembered the scene she had glimpsed through the paving-crack; and how real it had seemed. How much more real than any dream.

She looked at her reflection in a nearby shop window, seeing herself in the darkened glass, her backpack over one shoulder. Her hair stood out in crazy spikes; her face was smudged with woodsmoke. She came a little closer and saw that, behind the glass, the window display was overrun with the same vegetation she had seen at the Tube entrance; brambles, and bindweed, and Russian vine, and something that might have been hawthorn. Some kind of a Hallowe'en display, thought Fay, seeing rose hips and blackberries growing against the dusty glass. Maybe some kind of conceptual art installation. Maybe it was Fashion Week, and this was some new way of selling clothes. She looked closer and saw that among the vines, there was indeed an array of evening wear, but the dresses looked old and neglected, and there were cobwebs in the lace; a layer of dust on the sequins.

She moved to the next shop window, which seemed to be a jeweller's. But here, too, there were creepers and vines growing up against the glass; there was dust on the display cases and the velvet lining, and the necklaces, bracelets and rings were all but obscured by sprays of bramble and autumn leaves.

Fay moved past the jeweller's shop, feeling her heartbeat quicken. Every shop she passed was the same; overgrown with creepers and vines, or branches bearing hips and haws, or thorny clusters of dust-grey sloes. She started to run. Her feeling of dread and her aching muscles drove her to it, and as she ran past the darkened shops – Waterstones, its display of books scattered like heaps of fallen leaves; Fortnum's, its display of gilded biscuit tins and bottles and chocolates all tangled with briars and foxgloves and rose – she saw that *all* the shops were the same; their windows dark and overgrown, gleefully bursting with baleful life. Some had broken windows, with scattered fragments of glass on the ground, allowing the creepers and brambles and vines to cascade out into the street. Fay saw a cluster of blackberries growing from a crack in a wall, picked one, popped it in her mouth. The taste was sharp and wild and strong, nothing like the blackberries she bought in shops.

She remembered a snatch of folklore; that at Michaelmas, the Devil spits on autumn's last crop of blackberries, making them bitter and poisonous. Even so, she took another handful of berries. They were not exactly *good*, and yet the taste of them was compelling. They tasted of smoke, and Bonfire Night, and cheap wine, and burned sugar. And they tasted *real* – more real than anything else on that silent street. Reaching Bond Street Station at last, Fay noticed that it too was closed off – and here too there were creepers and vines growing out of the entrance.

That decided it, she thought. Whatever had happened to the Tube, the road was still there, and she knew the way home. She turned back and started to run, slowly at first, then settling into a faster pace. At first her muscles were stiff from a night spent on the London streets, but she soon found her natural rhythm, and the pavement felt good against her feet. Back along Piccadilly she ran, then across the deserted square and up Shaftesbury Avenue. The autumn leaves that papered the ground made brittle, desperate sounds as she passed. Otherwise, it was eerily still. No sound of traffic, no sirens, no voices, no taxis, no passers-by – and now as she ran she realized that apart from the leaves, there was no litter on the road; not even a sweet wrapper. Running past the theatres she saw that the lights were still out on the billboards, and the posters and fliers were faded and torn, and that here and there were creepers and vines growing out of the doorways.

This time she did not stop to look, but quickened her pace and ran faster. The wind was strangely warm, and smelt of sage and samphire, and fallen leaves, and windfall apples, and blackberries. *Even the air is different today*, thought Fay. *It smells of the woods in autumn. I am lost in the wild woods, except that the woods look like London.*

By now she was approaching Euston Road. There, at least, would be people, she thought. But turning onto the carriageway, she saw no sign of life; no traffic; no litter but fallen leaves; not even a single pedestrian. And here, too, was that scent on the wind, that wind

that seemed so strangely warm, a scent that reminded her of the woods, a distillation of spices and leaves left to moulder and crumble and rot, and beyond it, the salty tang of the sea. And rolling in the gutter, Fay saw something that looked like a child's red ball, coming towards her, blown by the wind—

She stopped to retrieve it. It wasn't a ball. It was a single, flawless, red rose, tumbled and travelling with the wind. No florist's bloom, but an old-fashioned rose, packed with scented petals. Fay held it to her face. It smelt of summer and of endings. The wind must have blown it off a bush, in a churchyard, maybe, somewhere on the Euston Road. She tucked it carefully into her backpack, taking care not to crush the petals. Daisy always loved roses, she thought. The scented ones were her favourites. And Fay had always meant to plant a rose bush by her daughter's grave, but the task of choosing just one had been too much for her. There were so many, their names as enticing as their colours: Albertine; Grand Siècle; Autumn Damask; Madame Alfred Carrière. They sounded like ladies-in-waiting from some old French fairy-tale. But some part of her knew that once she had chosen a rose bush and planted it over Daisy's grave, she would have taken another step towards saying goodbye for ever. And Fay did not want to say goodbye. Not even with the pain of her loss like a tangle of thorns in her heart, remembering Daisy was all she had, and was better by far than forgetting her.

Once more she started to run down the road. Home was barely ten minutes away. And however alien London had become, home was still home, and meant safety. Home was where she and Allan had lived, in that little house near King's Cross with the patchy central heating; home was where Daisy had been conceived; where her childhood room stayed untouched, her toys and dolls all put away, her bed remade and aired every week, with flowers at her bedside. Home was where you went when nothing else in the world made sense, and all you wanted to do was curl up under a blanket and sleep until the stars began to fall and all the world was ashes.

But when Fay finally got to King's Cross, it was overgrown with weeds, and brambles grew across the road, and elders from the clock tower. And beyond that, there were no houses at all, except for some derelict buildings, roofless and empty and vaulted with trees and spreading Virginia creeper, and buddleia, and sycamore, and creeping scarlet roses.

London Beyond

≈

*'For da king o Ferrie we his daert,
Has pierced your lady to da hert.'*

Child Ballad no. 19: *King Orfeo*

One

For a long time, Fay stared at the forest that had been King's Cross. Some of the trees looked very old – a hundred and fifty years or more – and there were birds among the branches; magpies and starlings and jackdaws and crows. The wall between what had been York Way and the railway station still stood, although it was pitted and almost obscured under a curtain of creeper, and there was a narrow path running alongside it, leading into the forest.

Fay had long since ceased to tell herself that she was dreaming. If Daisy could be dead, she thought, then anything was possible. She came closer to the path, which was more like a tunnel overhung with branches and vines and strong brown twists of briar. Some of the briars still bore a few ripening blackberries, although most of the fruit had dried on the branch, and Fay picked and ate them, less out of hunger than out of a strange compulsion. It *was* enchanted fruit, after all. Perhaps, like the madcap, it opened doors.

She remembered Alberon's words to Mabs: *We'll find her again in London Beyond.* London Beyond. Was this where he had meant? Whatever had happened, she told herself, Alberon was a part of it. Fay knew she had to find him again.

She looked into the tunnel of leaves. The path there was small and winding. And yet it looked clear. She was not the first to seek a way through the undergrowth. She looked over her shoulder towards the deserted station, where the clock tower was overgrown with bindweed and roses. On the side of the building, someone had sprayed the phrase: MY PLAID AWAY in a wild, exuberant script. And the clock had stopped at 4.03 – the time at which she had received the call that Daisy had taken her own life—

What was it Alberon had said? *She sleeps in the hall of the Hallowe'en King.* At the time, Fay had barely heard him; the sight of Daisy asleep in the woods had taken up all her attention. But now his words came back to her like the rose on the wind: *She sleeps in the hall of the Hallowe'en King, and nothing you do here can wake her.*

Nothing you do <u>here</u> can wake her. Why not just *nothing can wake her*?

Because things have changed, she told herself. *Because the world is different now. Because I stepped on a crack and fell into a realm of magic.*

And at that thought, she stepped onto the path through the wilderness, into London Beyond.

TWO

A few steps onto the overgrown path, and it was already darker. Thick vegetation surrounded her in every shade of autumn. Light filtered through like stained glass in a narrow chapel of rest, and the wind was like plainsong through the leaves, whispering and calling. There were roses growing up into the canopy over her head: most of them had gone to seed, sending out sprays of rose hips, but there were still some dark-red blooms adding their scent to that of the leaves carpeting the forest floor.

The roses were barbed with wicked thorns, clutching at Fay's clothes and hair. And yet the path stayed clear enough, though walled in thickly from both sides, as it led her into the heart of the woods that now grew over Battlebridge. From time to time she could

hear birds, or see insects – jewelled beetles and moths
– crawling in the undergrowth. Fay remembered how
Peronelle and Cobweb and Moth had turned into
clouds of butterflies. Where were Alberon and his
friends now? Were they the only other people left in
this world? And how could she ever find them again
in this overgrown version of London?

And then she heard a sound from afar, like that of
a musical instrument. A horn, thought Fay, its mellow
tone both sweet and wild. It seemed to be coming from

somewhere ahead; beyond the urban forest. She heard it only once, and yet felt strangely drawn to the music. Someone was near. She was not alone. She followed the path towards the sound, quickening her pace as much as the undergrowth allowed and, after a time, emerged into a kind of clearing.

On one side of the clearing was the wall that ran alongside York Way. She saw a row of arches choked with vegetation, and beyond that the railway; the overhead lines now garlanded with bindweed. Trumpet-shaped flowers and heart-shaped leaves cascaded over signals and points, and there were railway carriages, now covered with moss and hanging vines. On the other side was forest, a little less dense than the patch through which she had crossed, with ruined buildings and ancient trees rising up out of the undergrowth.

The clearing itself was concrete, broken in many places, with dandelions and buddleia growing out of the cracks. A number of tags and slogans had been spray-painted on the ground, but the colours were old and faded. One read: THE KIDS FROM FAE, and beyond it, on the far side of clearing, lay an enormous tiger.

For a moment, Fay was pinned to the spot. A wave of adrenalin washed over her, and it was almost more than she could do to stop herself from running. But how could she outrun a tiger? *Don't behave like prey*, she thought. *Move slowly, with confidence.* She wondered whether to turn back into the thicket, but told herself that she would stand more of a chance if she stayed in the open. *Besides*, she thought, *I heard a horn*.

She started to move, very slowly, edging away from the tiger. The tiger watched her, motionless, except for the very tip of its tail, which twitched to and fro like the second hand of a watch with a dying battery. It was a very large tiger, radiant with health and life. It looked well-fed. Fay almost laughed. *A tiger, here in London?*

But this is London Beyond, she thought. *Anything is possible.*

The tiger shifted position. The arc of the tail grew wider. It stretched out a lazy forepaw, extending claws like grappling hooks. Fay was struck by how closely the creature resembled a domestic cat. *Daisy always wanted a cat*, she thought. *Why didn't we get one?* A low vibration reached her ears: the animal was purring.

Fay quickened her pace a little, heading towards the railway.

The tiger slowly rose to its feet. Each paw was the size of a footstool, upholstered in autumnal fur. The purr was a less of a sound than a tremor that moved through the concrete, that made the leaves shiver, that froze the sun. And now the tiger began to move, very slowly, towards her. It looked like an illustration in a Victorian children's book; every whisker perfectly rendered. And yet there was something unreal about it; something she could not identify. Maybe it was the mere fact of its presence, here in the concrete clearing, but Fay could not rid herself of the thought that she'd missed something obvious.

Fay was sure it could hear the quickening of her heart. Three seconds and the urge to run would be impossible to resist; three seconds and she would be prey, running helplessly from Death—

And then she saw a little girl standing by the tiger's side; standing so close that a swipe of a paw might erase her from the world. She looked about seven years old, and was wearing an adult's overcoat so large that it trailed behind her, the sleeves rolled up so far that her thin brown arms stuck out like twigs. She did not seem at all afraid, and in spite of her own fear, Fay found herself instinctively moving to protect her.

'Turn around slowly,' she said. 'Don't run. Running makes you look like prey.'

The little girl looked at Fay, and laughed. 'He won't hurt you,' she said. She had the same accent as Alberon and his friends; an accent that might have

been regional, but which Fay still could not quite place. She put her hand on the tiger's flank and the tiger licked it. 'Look,' said the child. 'He won't hurt us. Come and see.'

Fay stared at the child and her tiger. The animal's pads were large enough to cover the whole of the little girl's head. But the child seemed so certain of herself, one hand in the tiger's fur, the other extended to welcome Fay. The heavy purring intensified. The whole of the tiger's flank vibrated softly, like an engine.

She looks like Daisy, Fay thought. Daisy had been blonde as a child, and this girl was very dark, but her expression was the same mixture of curiosity and sweetness. And yet there was something odd about her; something faintly troubling in the way she she spoke and moved.

'What's your name?' said Fay at last.

The child shook her head. 'Don't have one,' she said.

'Is the tiger... yours?' asked Fay.

'Of course not,' said the little girl with reproach. 'Tigers don't belong to people. But he *is* my friend.'

'Oh. What's his name?'

'Tigers don't have names,' she said. 'They don't need them. None of us do.'

'Us?' said Fay.

'The travelling folk.'

That makes a sort of sense, thought Fay. Alberon and his friends had been travellers, at least of a kind. Perhaps she too was a traveller, caught between the London she knew and this overgrown, empty world. 'Where are they now, these travelling folk?'

'Everywhere.' The child made a gesture that took in the sky, the undergrowth, the trees, the broken buildings.

'Surely you don't live here all alone. Where are your parents?' said Fay.

Once more the child made a gesture, part shrug and part dismissal, as if the very idea of having parents was ludicrous. 'Don't have 'em. Don't need 'em.' She stroked the tiger's glossy flank. 'We don't live like tame folk. We don't have names, or families. We have fur and wings and teeth. We have roots and branches.'

'So where do you travel to?' said Fay. 'And do you know a man called Alberon?'

The little girl looked incredulous. 'You don't know much, do you?' she said. 'No, he isn't one of ours. He has more names than the Old Man himself. And he's nothing but trouble.'

The tiger gave a low growl, as if in agreement – or warning.

'It's OK,' said the little girl. Then, addressing Fay,

she said: 'We like to keep ourselves to ourselves. We don't get involved with the Silken Folk. You shouldn't either. They'll mess with your mind.' She put her small brown hand on Fay's arm. 'You don't belong here, my Lady,' she said. 'Go back before something happens.'

The tiger's purring resumed. Its eyes were a deep and luminous gold, flecked with dancing motes of light, and Fay had the strangest impression that it knew what she was thinking. And then, as she looked at the sunlight against the broken concrete, she realized what had troubled her about the little nameless girl. Neither she nor the tiger cast the slightest shadow.

Three

When Daisy's father died, she began to dream of a being called the Shadowless Man. For nearly a year she had dreamed of him; a tall man, pale and all in black, wearing a coat that was lined with eyes that blinked and glittered in the dark. Fay could only speculate on what had summoned the Shadowless Man, but the dreams had stopped when the pavement game had taken over Daisy's life; only returning nine years later, when the shadow of her depression had begun to creep over everything.

Of course, there was no such person as the Shadowless Man, Fay had told her. He was a symbol of something else, with his stern pale face and his coat of eyes. And yet, the dreams kept coming, growing ever more potent, ever more real, until the day she ended her life, only to exist in dreams.

But now dreams and reality seemed to have changed places. London had become the dream, and London Beyond the reality. And here was a child with no shadow, who might cast some light on the mystery.

'I can't go back. Not yet,' she said. 'I'm looking for my daughter. I know it sounds crazy. I thought she was gone. But I saw her last night, in the bluebell wood, through the cracks in the pavement.'

And she told the child all she remembered: of Alberon and his group of friends; the madcap; the light through the pavement cracks. She even showed her the red rose that had come to her on the wind, and mentioned the sound of the hunting horn that had led her through the forest.

The child listened attentively, but showed no surprise at the story. Then she looked at the tiger. 'Well?'

The tiger seemed to consider her words. Then it spoke, addressing Fay in a voice which held the hint of a purr: 'Madcap. That would do it, o Queen. Madcap is what brought you here.'

She said: 'Why do people keep calling me that?'

'You're Queen Orfeia,' the tiger said. 'Everyone knows that, Your Majesty.'

'But I'm *not* a Queen,' said Fay. 'And I've never been here before in my life. My name is Fay Orr. I'm from London.'

The tiger made a gesture that was oddly like a shrug. 'Whoever you were in London, Your Majesty, you're Queen Orfeia in London Beyond. Your singing is known throughout the Worlds; as clear as the call of the cuckoo.'

Fay said: 'I don't sing any more.'

'That's very wise,' said the tiger. 'And yet you might do well to remember some of the songs of the Nine Worlds. There's wisdom in an old wives' tale, and magic in a story.'

And in a beautiful baritone voice, the tiger began to sing. The words were a little different, but the tune was familiar: it was the same as the song Peronelle had sung to her the previous night; a night that now seemed as far away as Daisy, asleep in the bluebells.

The elphin knight sits on yon hill,
Bay, bay, lily bay.
He blows his horn both loud and shrill,
My plaid shall not be blown away.

My plaid away, my plaid away,
And o'er the hill and far away,
And far away to Norroway,
My plaid shall not be blown away.

Fay wanted to ask all kinds of things: about the song, what a plaid was, and about madcap, and Mabs and Alberon, and why the girl and her tiger seemed so sure she was Queen Orfeia. But all that really mattered, she thought, was Daisy, glimpsed through the pavement crack, and Alberon saying: *She sleeps in the hall of the Hallowe'en King, and nothing you do here can wake her.*

'Have you heard of the Hallowe'en King?' she said.

The little girl nodded. 'Of course,' she said. 'He lives far away, on the shore of the river Dream. Some call him Lord Death, the Harlequin, the Erl-King, or the Elphin Knight. Sometimes they call him the Shadowless Man.'

Fay felt her heart clench like a fist. 'I need to find him,' she said. 'I think he may have taken my daughter.'

The girl gave her a look combining surprise and pity. 'People don't *find* the Hallowe'en King,' she said. 'He finds *them*. Eventually.'

'Not me,' said Fay. 'I'm going to find *him*. Where is he? Do you know?'

The tiger yawned, showing a full set of sharp teeth. 'To reach the Hallowe'en King, Your Majesty, you must go into Nethermost London. But there is no madcap in London Beyond to help you on your journey. It only grows by the shore of Dream, under the cliffs of Damnation. And to travel as far as the court of the King, you'll have to take the Night Train.'

'The Night Train?'

'You heard its horn.'

Fay thought back to the sound she had heard; its low and musical command. It made a certain sense, she thought, for there still to be trains in London Beyond. 'So where do I find the Night Train?'

The travelling girl extended a hand across the stretch of concrete. Beyond it, through the arches, Fay could see down into a kind of decline of junction boxes, and signals, and points, and above it all a network of lines and cables like a spider's web, with carriages tumbled like children's toys, all tangled with bindweed and clematis and briar rose and Russian vine. Surely no trains could be running now. And yet she had heard the Night Train's horn. It must be down there, some-where.

'The Train leaves from Nethermost London,' said the tiger in its purring voice. 'The path there is dark, and the price is high. Obstacles and dangers abound. Beware false friends, and false promises. Most of all, beware the Silken Folk, and their hospitality. For if you take as much as a mouthful of the food of World

Below, you will never leave again, or hope to find your daughter.'

Fay moved towards the arches that marked the descent into the station. 'Which platform does the train leave from?' she said. 'And do I need a ticket?'

But when she turned back, the travelling girl and her tiger had already vanished.

Four

There was a flight of red-brick steps leading down into the station. Like everything else they were broken and overgrown and tangled with weeds, and there was more graffiti on the wall running alongside the banister. Among the many faded tags and graffiti, one in particular caught her eye. It was a faint, almost fey sky-blue, and read: SHE SLEEPS IN TIR NA NOG. Another, in the same faded blue, simply read YOUR DAISY.

Fay paused to touch the inscription: the paint was old, beginning to flake, and there were small white crystals growing out of the damp stone. She proceeded down the steps, taking care to avoid the tumbling coils of creeper, and finally reached the heart of the overgrown station.

Looking up, she could see the sky through a roof of broken glass; a sky unmarred by vapour trails or blurred by air pollution. The platforms and rail tracks were overrun with weeds; yellow ragwort and buddleia and great umbrels of giant hogweed that loomed over the leaf canopy. Fay noticed that the leaves were still green and the buddleia still in flower down here, as if she had left the autumn behind and was moving back towards summer, but all the trains left on the tracks were clearly long-abandoned. Some of the carriages had been knocked onto their sides, and some were filled with briars and vines, but nowhere could she see a sign of a working locomotive. On the concrete at her feet, someone had sprayed the familiar words: MY PLAID SHALL NOT BE BLOWN AWAY, in faded, silver spray. On one of the tumbled carriages, someone had scrawled the word: XANADU.

But Fay was not alone here. A sound from the buddleia bushes that grew around the platform suggested the presence of animals. Something large, by the sound of it – Fay thought of the tiger, and shivered.

'Who's there?' she said.

The sound – a furtive rustling – came once more from the undergrowth. Fay approached, and saw a face peering out of the bushes. It was one of Alberon's folk; the one with the eyepatch and the tattoos, Moth.

Another face appeared alongside: it was the girl, Cobweb.

'Were you following me?' said Fay.

The two figures parted the undergrowth and moved into the open. Fay saw that Moth was wearing a strapless dress and a pair of Dr Martens boots; Cobweb, without her wheelchair now, was wearing pink legwarmers and a hooded sweatshirt, bearing the slogan: 4 EVA FAE.

She smiled. 'Of course, Your Majesty.'

Moth bowed. 'Well met, Queen Orfeia. King Alberon sends his compliments, and begs the delight of your company.'

Last night they had looked like homeless folk, but here by day in London Beyond, the pair seemed altogether different. It was not simply the change of clothes, or the absence of Cobweb's wheelchair; it was something more than that. A luminous quality to their skin, which was smooth and acorn-brown; a fleeting shimmer around them, like midges in the sunlight. Like the girl and her tiger, Fay saw, the pair of them cast no shadow.

'King Alberon?' Fay repeated, remembering the madcap smoke, and how they had danced together. That seemed so far away to her now, and so very long ago. And yet – that he should be a king here was no more surprising than anything else. After all, she told herself, this world was like a pack of cards; it seemed to be filled with kings and queens. But the tiger had warned her: *beware false friends*. And hadn't the travelling girl told her Alberon was nothing but trouble?

'I'm sorry,' she said. 'I don't have time. I have to take the Night Train.'

Moth and Cobweb exchanged glances. 'That train

is not for the living,' said Moth. 'The price of a ticket is death, and those who take it only travel one way.'

'I have to,' said Fay. 'The Hallowe'en King has my daughter.'

'Then come to the court of King Alberon,' urged Cobweb. 'He knows the way to the Night Train. And there will be banqueting, and song, and company befitting the occasion. And His Majesty would have you bedecked in raiment fit for your station.' And at these words, the unlikely pair gestured towards the undergrowth, and a luminous cloud of insects emerged, descending onto Fay's shoulders and arms. Some of them looked like bright green bees, others like tiny lacewings; and as they settled on her like a veil, Fay felt her clothing fall away, to be replaced almost instantly by something that felt like gossamer.

'Tailor bees, Your Majesty,' said Moth.

'Lacemakers,' said Cobweb. 'Don't be afraid, Your Majesty. Just let your servants do their work.'

Fay, who had never been fearful of any kind of insect, watched the creatures with interest. The tailor bees and the lacemakers seemed to be *weaving* at incredible speed; creating a delicate webwork of silk, draped like the finest crêpe de Chine. Moth made another gesture, and now a third kind of insect swarmed to join the lacemakers and the tailor bees. They looked like shiny beetles, gleaming in the sunlight, and as Fay watched, she saw that they were fixing particles of something that looked like tiny flecks of mica between the strands of woven silk.

'Sequin bugs,' said Cobweb. 'To make a gown befitting a queen.'

Fay tried to protest as the tailor bees severed the straps of her backpack; cut away her running clothes, her leggings and her laces. She had no time for adornments. She had to find the Night Train. Anything else, she told herself, was a dangerous distraction. But as the silken gown took shape, she was unable to stop herself from watching in fascination. Woven to fit her perfectly; artfully draped in its many layers; in spite of its gossamer lightness, the fabric was deceptively strong. It shone like iridescent moiré, and now she saw that in the silk there were patterns of flowers and leaves, frosted into the warp and weft of the fabric like flowers on winter glass.

It took only minutes to create, the tailor bees humming imperiously, and the sequin bugs trundling busily around the neckline and the sleeves. Fay could feel them in her hair, moving and adjusting the strands, weaving them into an intricate coronet of jewelled braids. Then, when their work was complete, the creatures all took wing and dispersed,

illuminating the air with their wings so that everything was rainbow.

Cobweb and Moth had averted their eyes. Now they watched again as Fay moved towards one of the abandoned railway carriages and tried to look at herself in the glass. Even in dusty reflection, she thought, the result was astonishing.

'And now, your carriage awaits,' said Moth.

Fay tore herself away from the sight of her transformation.

'My carriage?' she said. 'I'm sorry, I can't. I told you, I'm taking the Night Train.'

Moth smiled. 'Of course, Your Majesty. But King Alberon knows the Night Train. He himself has taken it, all the way to Tír na nÓg and over the sea to Norrowa. Few living men can say the same. He can help, Your Majesty.'

Fay thought for a moment. She needed a friend. This world was too full of mysteries and dangerous transformations. And besides, it had been Alberon who had led her here in the first place. He owed her an explanation.

She looked down once more at her silken gown, so artfully draped and richly adorned; looked into the dusty window-glass at her crown of braided hair. A banquet, she thought; with music, and company fit for the occasion. It sounded both lovely and dangerous, and yet, perhaps, if she went along, she might learn the secret to Daisy's return...

She looked at Cobweb and Moth. 'Very well,' she said, and smiled. 'Take me to King Alberon.'

Five

The carriage Moth had promised her was precisely that: an abandoned rail car, windows smashed, and draped with bindweed and spider's webs. Someone, decades ago, had scrawled HE PLAYED DA GABBER REEL in rose-coloured spray paint over one dull and dusty flank.

Moth smiled at Fay and beckoned her in. 'Your carriage, Your Majesty.'

Fay picked up her pack and cautiously looked inside the carriage. It smelt of age, and dust, and weeds, and cracked and ancient leather. How could it travel anywhere? There wasn't even an engine, she thought. And yet things were not as they seemed in this place, where tigers talked, and bees wove silken fabrics more intricate than the most exquisite brocade. Holding the skirts of her gown away from the clutching briars, she chose the seat that seemed least damaged, and sat there, with her pack on her knees. Moth and Cobweb joined her, taking their places by the door. Cobweb pulled out a silver cigarette case and lit a small, brown cigarette, using an old-fashioned lighter almost as large as the case itself. The smoke coiled into the air like vines. Fay caught the scent of madcap.

She opened her mouth to comment, but already something was happening. As the madcap filled the space, the inside of the carriage seemed to shift and shimmer. At first Fay thought that maybe the smoke was affecting her eyes, but it seemed as if the carriage had been transformed, to become a lavish interior. The cracked and faded leather seats had changed to elegant armchairs with cushions of midnight-blue velvet. The ceiling was painted in the same rich colour, and gilded with thousands of silver stars. The dangling briars had become chandeliers filled with lighted candles, and there was a scent of patchouli and rose and sandalwood and spices.

'Glamours, Your Majesty,' said Cobweb, whose pink sweatshirt and legwarmers had now become a brightly coloured tunic of something that looked like feathers. 'Even here, in London Beyond, our people like to go unseen.'

'Too many enemies,' said Moth. 'Too many spies and predators.'

Moth, too, had changed, Fay noticed. Gone were the eyepatch and the tattoos. Gone too, was the illusion of something more or less human. Now a row of gleaming eyes shone out from a mask of feathers, and the intricate designs that Fay had taken for tattoos now seemed to be natural markings, grey and brown and russet against the downy, luminous skin.

The carriage was moving, she realized; almost soundlessly, on the rails. How this could be, with no engine, she had no idea, and yet through the windows she could see the sooty arches of King's Cross. The carriage entered a tunnel; for a moment Fay saw light reflected against the seeping stone. Through an arch she saw a glimpse of torches burning, then darkness fell like a velvet curtain over the scene. The carriage was moving so silently that Fay had no idea of its speed, and so when it emerged into sunlight she was startled to see the scenery passing in a blur of fitful colours. They had somehow left the rails, and were moving through a stretch of unfamiliar countryside. Trees flashed past, their trailing branches slapping against the glass, and Fay could see that their leaves were young and green, as if in springtime.

She barely had time to take in the view when they

entered another tunnel. This time, when they emerged, it was into a scene of unfamiliar streets, with a sky like faded roses reflected in towers of grasshopper glass. Then another tunnel, and they emerged into a soft grey mist, in which great, delicate structures, like cranes, seemed to stride on endless legs.

Leaning forward, she tried to see what kind of engine was pulling the carriage. But when she put her face to the glass, she saw, not a locomotive, but something that made her pull back with a gasp. The carriage was being pulled by a quartet of creatures that looked to be something between a flying horse and a giant hummingbird moth. All were a curious silver-grey, with great wings blurring furiously, and powerful flanks, and narrow heads, topped with plume-like antennae. A complicated harness kept the strange creatures under control, and as Fay watched she saw that there was someone holding the reins, perching high above the team in a tiny, precarious seat. Purple hair flew angrily. Lightning cracked from their fingers. It was Peronelle.

'Have no fear, Your Majesty,' said Cobweb. 'The hellride is nearly over.'

Hellride, thought Fay. An apt term, having seen their driver. The carriage was entering another of those tunnels. Darkness, now stitched with tiny lights, surrounded the railway carriage. There was no sensation of movement; no sense of how much time had passed. Only the glow from the candles illuminated the carriage. And then the door opened, and she saw someone in the doorway; a tall, pale man with long hair, richly dressed in dark velvet and wearing a crown of white gems that shone like the light of the full moon on ice.

For a moment Fay was unsure of the tall, pale man's identity. He looked somewhat familiar, and yet she did not know him until he smiled; a warm and familiar smile that seemed born of a lifetime's acquaintance.

'Queen Orfeia. Well met,' he said. 'Welcome to London Beneath.'

It was Alberon.

Six

Alighting from the carriage, Fay found herself in a passageway lined with tiny, stuttering lights. They looked like strings of fairy lights, but closer observation showed them to be clusters of glowing insects.

'Torchflies, Your Majesty,' said Moth, who was already busy unharnessing the moth-horse creatures that had drawn the carriage. Peronelle was hard at work, brushing down their dusty flanks, sending great clouds of luminescence into the air. The creatures were restless, their fluttering wings making a dry and thunderous sound, their plume-like feelers turning to Fay in eager curiosity. Now that she saw them more closely, Fay could see the death's-head pattern behind their heads, etched in soot on the dappled pelt that was neither fur nor feathers, but some hybrid of both.

Alberon took her hand and guided her down the passageway. 'I hope your journey was comfortable.'

Fay nodded. 'As hellrides go.'

He laughed, and she was struck by his charm, which was both warm and effortless. In London, his charm had already been clear; but here in London Beneath, it shone from him like a searchlight.

'You must be exhausted. Let me carry your purse.' He reached out to take her backpack. But Fay did not want to abandon her pack, which was all that remained of her previous life. Clinging to the broken strap, she shook her head. 'I'll keep it, thanks.'

The King's smile broadened. 'Of course, my Queen. If anyone can carry off a nylon backpack with an evening gown, you can. But at least let me offer you a drink.' He made a summoning gesture, and a crystal goblet appeared in his hand, containing a sparkling liquid that looked a little like champagne, but which glowed with a slight luminescence.

'Wine,' he said, 'from the nectar of a cactus flower that blooms only once, grown in the mountains of the Moon, filtered through crystal, and served on ice from beyond the land of the Northlights.'

Fay began to reach for the glass. But then she remembered the tiger's words, and its warning not to eat or drink of anything in London Beneath. And so she shook her head – with regret, for the wine smelt of sparklers and Bonfire Night, and shone like a jar of fireflies.

'Thanks. But I prefer to keep a clear head.'

Alberon dismissed the goblet with a casual wave of the hand. 'No matter,' he said, and, with a gesture into the dark, opened up the passageway into a magnificent hall, lit by a thousand chandeliers of filigree and grasshopper glass, from which a million torchflies glowed and gleamed and flickered.

The ceiling was unimaginably high, disappearing into the dark, and the walls were illuminated with veins of some kind of shining mineral, which sparkled as it caught the light, casting reflections over a floor of butterflies' wings in amber. Silver incense burners were scattered at intervals around the hall, releasing a scent of musk-rose, and green patchouli, and ambergris. All around there were delicate chairs of sandalwood and ebony and teak and coromandel, with cushions of silken brocade, moth's wing, and gleaming dragonfly leather.

And in the centre of the hall there was a table, broad and long, covered with damask and silverware and goblets of fine crystal, and set with innumerable dishes of the most exquisite kind.

There were great towers of gleaming fruit, and frosted grapes, and persimmons, and silver platters of venison, and roast fowl stuffed with chestnuts, and fishes with their tails in their mouths, and sea urchins on beds of dill weed. There were dishes of roast asparagus and artichokes and truffles, and bowls of delicate summer greens mixed with edible flowers. There were bowls of nuts and seeds, and marchpane, candied roses, and cakes of all kinds, laden with fruit or gilded, or iced, and delicate as honeycomb. Then there were strange, exotic things: honeyed earwigs and grasshopper legs, and roasted silkworms served on a bed of caterpillar marshmallow. And all around there were noble guests, and servants, bearing silver trays of canapés and drinks of all kinds in glasses adorned with butterflies' wings and multicoloured flowers.

The King beckoned a servant – a feathered creature with many eyes and a long proboscis, a little like Moth – who was bearing a silver tray of tiny canapés.

'My Queen, you must be hungry,' he said. 'I have collected together the best the Nine Worlds have to offer: fruits from the southernmost islands; abalones from the One Sea; nectar from the shores of Dream; spices from the Outlands. Or perhaps you would prefer to try the heart of a lovebird, a nightingale's tongue, or the flesh of the very last dodo?'

Fay shook her head. 'I'm not hungry,' she said. 'I came because I need your help.'

He smiled. 'You want the Night Train.'

Fay looked at him. 'You knew?'

'Of course. This is London Beneath, my Queen. I know everything that happens here. I know you seek the Hallowe'en King, to beg for the return of your Daisy.' He stopped to take a canapé of butterflies' tongues in a hazelnut shell. 'But I beg you, lay aside your quest until the morning. Tonight there will be music, and dancing, and song from all the tribes of World Below. And if you have no appetite for food or drink or merriment, then at least give me your company, so that no one will say King Alberon failed in his duty as a host.'

Fay looked around at the many richly clad guests in their masks of coloured feathers. Some of them had butterfly wings, or armour of dragonfly leather, cloaks of embroidered spider-silk, or coats of sequin beetles. Overlooking the hall, cut into the rock high above, Fay saw a minstrels' gallery, lit by a magnificent chandelier of torchflies. There were stag beetle horns, and spider's-web harps, and bumblebee drones, and grasshopper strings. A damselfly with a dulcimer sang in a high soprano voice in a language Fay could not identify, and yet could understand perfectly. And as she listened, more instruments joined in the chorus, more

voices joined the soloist and the music cascaded like broken crystal into the crowded banqueting-hall—

Alberon held out his hand. 'One dance.'

Fay thought of the words of the travelling girl, and of the tiger's warning. But a dance would surely do no harm, and the music was irresistible. And so she held out her hands to the King, and allowed him to draw her into his arms.

For a time, that was enough. She closed her eyes and allowed herself to be guided gently onto the floor. The music was strange and beautiful; the sounds both joyous and yearning. Alberon's hand rested on her waist; the other on her shoulder. Through the fabric of her dress she could feel the warmth of his fingers. They danced, Fay still clutching her pack, and the whole of the banqueting hall danced with them, chandeliers and musicians and guests, and tables and servants and dishes and lights, revolving like a kaleidoscope. From the silver incense-burners came the scent of roses. It was exhilarating, and yet something continued to trouble her. How had King Alberon known to expect her arrival? And why were he and the rest of his folk so certain she was somebody else?

Alberon whispered into her ear: 'Perhaps it is *you* who should ask yourself why you are so certain you're not.'

Fay was alarmed. Had she spoken aloud? It seemed to her that she had not, and yet somehow he'd heard her thoughts. The scent of roses intensified, and Fay began to feel the same strange sense of dislocation that she had felt in Piccadilly Circus. Colours blurred into musical notes; faces took on strange aspects. The dance, so slow at first, was beginning to feel like another hellride.

'I've never been here before,' she said.

'Oh but you have,' said Alberon. 'You may not remember your dreams, my Queen, but your dreams remember you.'

'Am I dreaming now?' said Fay.

Alberon smiled. 'No, my Queen. Now, at last, you are awake.'

Hellride

≈

'Noo come ye in inta wir ha,
An come ye in among wis a'.'
Now he's gaen in inta der ha,
An he's gaen in among dem a'.

Child Ballad no. 19: *King Orfeo*

One

'There once was a King of the Silken Folk, long ago, and far away. He was a powerful ruler, but he was also a selfish husband. His wife, Queen Orfeia, longed for a child, but the King was oblivious to her need, impatient with her sadness. And so she turned to Dream to provide the comfort that her man would not, and in its secret depths she sought the answer to her loneliness.'

Alberon smiled, and the gold in his eyes spun and sparkled like fireworks.

'Dream is a river,' he went on, 'that runs through every one of the Worlds. It shows us reflections of our lives. It carries them downstream. And sometimes those dreams become islands; and sometimes they become whole Worlds, bright and insubstantial as a bubble in sunlight.'

Fay tried to close her eyes; to escape Alberon's irresistible charm. But the dance, and the lights, and the feel of his hand on her waist and the nape of her neck kept her in his power, and the story kept unfolding.

'The Queen had powers of her own, and glamours to rival those of the King, and her dreams were equally powerful, building a wall between her and the life she shared with him. And in time, she came to believe that the dream-world she had built for herself was the truth, and her real life nothing but fantasy. She sought out ever stronger draughts to help her reach that joyful place. And she spent her days and nights in Dream, sleeping ever more and more, until at last she vanished from the real world altogether, and was lost – for ever, they thought – in that world of her own creation.

'But the King had finally understood his part in his wife's disappearance. He was cruel, and selfish, and bad, but he loved her, and was deeply ashamed. And so he went in search of her, combing the islands and skerries of Dream, hoping to find his lost Queen among all the flotsam of the Worlds. But when at last he found her – after many years of searching – she did not recognize him at all, and simply retreated into her dream, so that the King was left alone, grieving; inconsolable.'

Alberon reached to touch Fay's hair, and continued: 'And yet he waited, hoping that one day she would return to him. Meanwhile, in her dream, the Queen fell in love with a man of the Folk, and had a daughter whom she loved more than anything she had ever loved in the waking world.'

'It wasn't a dream,' Fay managed to say. 'Daisy was real. So was Allan.'

'Of course they were,' said Alberon. 'Anything that can be dreamed is true. And yet they belonged to the river, and the river took them back in the end. And so the Queen was left dreaming, alone, without her glamours or memory, while over the water, the King looked on, powerless to reach her. Until one day, in his despair, he went in search of the Oracle. The Oracle was old, and filled with ancient malice and hatred. It dwelt in the heart of World Below in a roaring cradle of fire, but it was cunning, learned, and wise, and it was bound to tell the truth to anyone who petitioned it.

'The road to the Oracle was long and filled with untold dangers. And yet the King endured them, and fought his way to the Oracle, to ask how the Queen could be released, for her dream had become a nightmare.

'The Oracle smiled from its cradle of fire. Its face

was all age and all malice. Its lips were sewn shut, and yet it spoke to him in a baleful whisper:

'"To free your lady," the Oracle said, "you must find the madcap mushroom, which grows in the caves on the shores of Dream, under the cliffs of Damnation. Correctly used, it opens up the doors between the Worlds, and will allow your Queen to pass between the realms of Dream and Waking. To reach the place where madcap grows, you will have to take the Night Train to the Kingdom of Death, where the Hallowe'en King, on his bone-white throne, watches the Worlds through his one living eye. But those who enter the Kingdom of Death are seldom allowed to leave it. The Hallowe'en King demands a price – be sure you are willing to pay it."

'"More than willing," said the King. "I thank you for your wisdom."

'The Oracle gave its twisted smile, and sank back into its cradle of fire. "I speak as I must," it told him. "And I cannot be silent."'

TWO

Fay listened to Alberon's story as the room circled faster and faster. Her head was filled with colours and lights; her stomach with barbed wire and butterflies. The scent of roses was maddening; it filled the air like a choking rain. And still they danced on, the King leading her around the room with a strong hand in the small of her back, his dark eyes never leaving hers.

She wanted to tell him to stop, but the words somehow refused to take shape. Around her, the musicians, the guests, the tables laden with glassware and sweets had taken on a nightmarish cast. She felt both numb and excruciatingly sensitive to everything; even the fabric of her gown seemed to be filled with briars and thorns.

She clutched at Alberon's coat. 'Please.'

He smiled, and the dancing lights in his eyes reflected the gleam of his jewelled crown. 'Are you unwell, my Lady?' he said, guiding her towards one of the chairs of gilded coromandel. 'Drink this. It will restore you.' And he handed her a goblet of wine that sparkled like a cup of stars.

Fay was just about to drink when she realized the trickery. She put down the wine untasted, and, still distressed and disoriented, said the first words that came into her mind, the strange words of the tiger's song: *'My plaid shall not be blown away.'*

Alberon flinched. 'Who taught you that?'

'I forget who taught me,' said Fay. 'But there's wisdom in an old wives' tale, and magic in a story.'

Alberon smiled. 'You are indeed wise,' he said. His discomfort had lasted no more than a moment, but his eyes were still cautious. Fay took a breath and felt her dizziness begin to abate. The words of the song made no sense to her and yet, somehow, they had power.

Alberon said: 'I hope my tale has not caused you any kind of distress. Believe me, it was not my intention to make you uncomfortable in any way.'

Fay returned his smile. The interruption, brief as it was, had given her time to recover. She touched the strap of her backpack, which she had

been clutching throughout the dance. *It's real*, she told herself. *I brought it here from London*.

So *this* was why King Alberon had tried to take her pack away. It was a reminder of who she was. It was her only link to her world. Once more she thought of the words of the song – *My plaid shall not be blown away* – and thought that maybe she knew their meaning, after all.

Summoning all her composure, she said: 'Not at all, Your Majesty. It would take far more than a tale to make me doubt my sanity. But please continue with your enchanting tale of the Night Train, and the Hallowe'en King.'

Once more Alberon smiled, and his eyes gleamed in appreciation. 'As my Queen desires,' he said. 'I live to serve at her pleasure.' And, taking his seat beside her, he continued his story, while around them the torchflies flickered and burned, and the dancers spun ever more merrily.

Three

'The easiest way for a living man to board the Night Train is to die,' said Alberon with a slow smile. 'But the King was not ready to give up his life, and so he sought another way. The way to all the Worlds is Dream, and Dream is the mother of Story, and it was through stories and dreams that the King found a way to fulfil his desire.'

Alberon sipped his wine, and went on: 'The King knew many old stories and songs, and his voice was renowned throughout the Worlds. Songs can open doors, he knew, and stories make connections. And so he went into World Below and sat beside the railway tracks, and sang a song of love and loss, and waited for the Night Train.

'He sang of King Orfeo, a legendary King of the

Folk, known throughout the Nine Worlds for his skill with every musical instrument. King Orfeo had a wife, taken much too soon by Lord Death to his hall in World Below. So the King, in his despair, travelled to the Land of the Dead, and begged Death for his wife's release.

'Lord Death looked down from his bone-white throne, in his crown of dead man's ivory. His living eye was blue as the sky; his dead eye dark as for ever.

'"What will you give me in return?" he said with his twisted half-smile.

'"Anything I own," said the King. "Gold, and lands, and tapestries, and carpets from beyond the seas, and perfumes from the islands."

Lord Death laughed, and his living eye shone with terrible merriment. "I have no need of treasures," he said. "Gold and land have no currency here, nor gems, or wealth, or perfumes."

'King Orfeo looked around him at the dusty palace of Lord Death; its ivory floors; faded tapestries; vaulted, bone-white ceilings. Everything was silent here: the people were nothing but shadows. His wife was among those shadows, he knew, but she did not know him now, for when a mortal loses their shadow, they lose all of their memories.

'"Then let me play for you, my Lord. Music is my

currency. I can play a reel so gay that all the bones in this palace will dance; I can sing a song so true that even the dead will listen."

'Lord Death looked down from his bone-white throne, and his face was both handsome and cruel. "Then sing to me," he said with a smile. "And I will return your wife to you – but only if you can make me weep."

'So King Orfeo sang a song of love so sweet and true that Death himself was moved to sigh, and a single tear ran down the living side of his ruined face. And when it was over, from the shadows, he led forth a pale and beautiful woman: it was the wife of Orfeo.

"I promised you your wife," said Lord Death with his mocking half-smile. "And here she is. But her shadow remains in my Kingdom, for ever and without release."

'And so Orfeo took his wife back into the waking World. But she did not know him, or herself, but walked with him as if in a dream, and would not eat, and would not drink, and looked at him with narrowed eyes, as if he were a stranger, for she had lost her shadow, and with it, all memory of her former life.

'"Do you not remember me, my love?" asked King Orfeo.

'The young woman only shook her head. "I was dreaming such a beautiful dream," she told the King,

with tears in her eyes. "I was in a land far away, over the seas to Norroway, and there I slept in a grass-green glade, all scented with summer roses."

'In vain, King Orfeo tried to coax his Queen into remembering their love. But he was a stranger to her now, and she would not be comforted. And so, in despair, he took her to the Oracle of World Below, which slumbered deep in its cradle of fire, all bound with runes and glamours.

'"How can I make her love me again?" Orfeo asked the Oracle.

'And the Oracle opened one eye and spoke:

> *When you can make me a cambric shirt,*
> *Every sage grows merry in time*
> *Without any seam or needlework*
> *Then will you be lovers again.*

'"How can that be?" asked Orfeo. "Is this a riddle? Is this a trick?"

'The Oracle gave its twisted smile.

> *When you can find me an acre of land,*
> *Every sage grows merry in time,*
> *Between the ocean and the sand*
> *Then will you be lovers again.*

'King Orfeo shook his head angrily. "Mock me you will not," he said. "Ask of me anything you will, but let us have no more of these riddles."

'The Oracle's dark eyes shone cruelly. "I speak as I must," it told him. "I speak as I must, and cannot lie:"

> *When you can walk shadowless at noon*
> *Every sage grows merry in time*
> *Hand in hand, once more you may*
> *Lovers be; together again.*

'And at these final words it sank back into its cradle of glamours and would not speak another word.

'And so King Orfeo took his Queen back into the land of the living, but the reunion brought him no happiness. His Queen stayed cold and sad and remote from that day till the end of their lives, and the King never played or sang again.'

King Alberon paused to finish his wine. 'Beware asking Death for a favour,' he said, 'lest Death be inclined to grant it. That is the moral of my tale, and the lesson is a harsh one.'

Four

As Alberon finished his goblet of wine, Fay looked once more at the banqueting hall. Everything had stopped as the King told the tale of Orfeo. Dancers, musicians, revellers all now stood in reverent silence: with feathered masks, furred faces and gowns of moth's-wing velvet. Few of them now looked human at all. Faceted eyes, plumed feelers, long beaks all turned to the royal couple.

'What a sad story,' said Fay with a smile that hid her deep and growing unease. 'And was the King of your story not discouraged from his quest?'

Alberon shook his head. 'He was not. He was a constant lover, even in the face of his lady's desertion.'

'It seems to me that his lady was somewhat

justified,' she said. 'But tell me: how did he manage to board the Night Train?'

Alberon smiled. 'I do apologize: my love of old tales can sometimes lead my tongue astray. My Queen, I understand that you prefer not to drink, or eat, or dance, but I beg of you, grant me the pleasure of hearing you sing, for I have heard tales of your marvellous voice, and, like Lord Death, I would hear it.'

At his words, the revellers all murmured their agreement. A figure standing behind them said: 'Much can be paid for with a song – as long as you choose the *right* song.' She turned and saw Mabs, in a long grey gown of embroidered moth velvet, her hair shining like starlight beneath a circlet of twisted silver. Behind her, she saw Peronelle – barely recognizable now but for the tumble of purple hair – watching her from behind a fan of jewelled lacewing and multicoloured moth's plume.

'Go for it. Sing,' said Peronelle, their smile revealing pointed teeth. 'Give us a song. A chorus will do. It's the least you can offer, my Queen, to thank us for our welcome.'

Fay hesitated. Where lay the harm? Surely a song could not be dangerous. And besides, she was eager to learn how the King had managed to board the Night Train.

'If I sing for you,' she said, 'will you promise to get me aboard the Night Train?'

King Alberon gave her a smile that was as warm as it was dangerous. 'If you still wish it, of course, my Queen. But sing me your song, for my heart is sore, and your voice may help to heal it.'

And so Fay took a breath and sang, for the first time since the loss of her daughter. She was out of practice, and her voice sounded lost and plaintive in the enormous banqueting hall. But she thought of the moment when Alberon had tried to take her backpack; the moment at which he had tried to trick her into taking a goblet of wine; and she sang the song the tiger had sung to her at the edge of the forest:

> *My plaid away, my plaid away,*
> *And o'er the hill and far away,*
> *And far away to Norroway,*
> *My plaid shall not be blown away.*

Why did she choose that particular verse? She did not know, except that it felt *powerful*, somehow, and that the words had surprised the King, and shaken his composure. They did not shake it now, she saw, with a touch of disappointment: his eyes were bright with amusement, as all around her the dancers stood, their

moths' wings fluttering eagerly, their plume-like feelers reaching out as if to feed on the music...

As Fay reached the end of the song, Alberon
clapped his approval. *'Brava, brava, brava!'* he cried,
and all his courtiers clicked their claws, and fluttered
their wings, and capered, and danced. 'And now you
must rest,' said Alberon, 'and take the Night Train in
the morning.'

Fay tried to protest, but King Alberon swept away
her objections. 'You must be exhausted,' he told her,
'after all your adventures. What you need is a good
night's sleep, in a bed of softest swansdown, with
sheets of the finest, whitest lawn, scented with sage
and lavender. Cobweb! Peronelle!' he called. 'You
shall see to her every desire, and sing her to sleep with
lullabies. My Queen,' he said, once more addressing
Fay, 'I bid you good night, and sweet slumbers. And in
the morning, if you so desire, we will speak once more
of the Night Train, and of your quest for your Daisy.'

Fay found herself being led away between Cobweb
and Peronelle. There were a hundred questions she
wanted to ask King Alberon but her head was spinning
with fatigue, and the thought of sleep was too tempting.
She allowed herself to be led into a cavern of majestic
proportions, with a floor of raw granite, gleaming with
gold, lit with clusters of torchflies, in which stood a

huge claw-footed bath and a bed with green brocade curtains. The bath was filled with hot water, and there were warm towels by a fire, and rose petals scattered over the floor and in the steaming water.

'Shall we help you disrobe, my Queen?' said Cobweb.

Fay shook her head.

'Then maybe we could sing to you? A lullaby, to soothe your sleep?'

Once more Fay shook her head. 'No, thank you. Leave me alone, please.'

Peronelle shot her a mischievous look. 'My Lady is an ungracious guest,' they said. 'What *does* he see in you?' And then they turned and left the room, singing an impudent fragment of song. Their voice, as high and sweet as a lark's, echoed down the passageway:

> *Queen Orfae went down to Mayfair,*
> *Every rose grows merry with time…*

Cobweb shot Fay a reproachful glance and followed Peronelle, leaving Fay alone in the beautiful chamber. The steam from the bath rose into the air, warm and irresistible. The torchflies glowed and glittered and shone like dancing wreaths of fairy lights.

She took off her brocade ballgown and stepped into

the water, feeling her aching muscles relax at last as she surrendered to the warmth. She closed her eyes and, for the first time since her daughter had died, felt a genuine sense of well-being; even almost of happiness. The water was scented with lavender and scattered with scarlet rose-petals. Eyes still closed, she breathed in the scent – and then she heard the sound of approaching footsteps, light as a cat's, and opened her eyes to see Mabs at her side, still in her moth-grey velvet gown and her crown of twisted silver.

'My Lady,' she whispered, 'have no fear. I'm here to help.' Little remained of the woman she'd been that night on Piccadilly. Now she seemed regal, luminous, her eyes as dark as the night sky.

'Help me?' Fay said. 'Why?'

Mabs lowered her voice still further. 'I don't have much time to explain,' she said. 'King Alberon knows everything that happens here in World Below. He wants you to forget your life, to remain here in his kingdom. So far you have resisted him, but if you want to leave this place, take nothing, give nothing, and most of all, do not give up your shadow.'

Fay looked around at the bedchamber; the warm and welcoming fire, the bed piled high with pillows and surrounded with hanging draperies.

'What do you mean?' she said.

'For everything you accept from him,' said Mabs, 'he steals one of your memories. Small things at first but soon you will find yourself losing days, and weeks, and years, until all that is left is Alberon – his face, his voice, his glamours – and your shadow, and with it your memory, and all that remains of your other life will fade away, so that you will be bound to stay in his world for ever.'

'But I haven't accepted *anything*,' protested Fay.

'Oh, but you did. A story. A song. A dance. These things all have power,' said Mabs.

'But that's impossible,' said Fay. 'How can a story have power?'

'Stories and songs are the language of Dream,' said Mabs. 'The oldest and most magical tongue. The bees discovered it, long ago, and carried it throughout the Worlds – all the Worlds of the honeycomb.'

'But he promised to help me find Daisy,' said Fay.

'And so he will, if you hold fast.' Mabs sighed. 'I have told you all I can to help you vanquish Alberon. Stories and songs are his currency, his power and his glamour. Riddles too – especially those. But they can be used against him, too – as long as you keep your wits about you.'

She looked behind her into a dark that was stitched with gleaming torchflies. 'I must go, my Lady,' she said. 'His servants and spies are everywhere. But keep your plaid safe, and your memories, even if they give you pain. Oh, and if you can' – she turned, light-footed, at the cavern's mouth – 'find out how King Orfeo came to lose his shadow.'

And then she was gone into the dark, her silver hair shining like starlight; the sound of her feet against the stone no louder than that of a moth's wing against the flame of a candle.

Five

Fay dried herself with one of the towels hanging by the fireplace. Mabs' visit had troubled her, and her sense of unusual well-being was gone. And yet in spite of this she felt better; more grounded, more true to herself. As if she had emerged from a cocoon of novocaine. The numbness was deceptive; hiding pain, not healing it.

Had Alberon charmed her somehow into forgetting her grief? Fay could almost believe he had. For a magical evening, she had... no, not quite *forgotten* her loss, but at least had felt the pain recede into something approaching acceptance. Was that what Mabs had meant when she said: *Keep your plaid safe, and your memories*? And what had she meant when she spoke of losing her shadow?

Fay dropped the towel and looked for her shadow on the chamber floor. In the soft light of the torchflies, it looked less distinct than usual. But that was just the light, she thought. There was no reason to believe that her shadow had lost definition. And yet – she looked at the four-poster bed with its curtains, its white linen sheets; its blanket of silk and swansdown. It looked like a ship, she told herself, tall enough to sail away across the sea to Norroway. What dreams would she dream in such a bed? What distant shores she would visit?

Her pack was still lying on the floor, looking old and out of place on the gleaming granite. She opened it and looked inside, hoping to find something to eat. She was very hungry now, having eaten nothing in twenty-four hours but a handful of blackberries. She found an apple, two cereal bars, and a bottle of water – enough to make a meal of sorts, without eating the food of London Beneath. She felt very tired, and longed to try the beautiful bed that looked like a ship but, remembering what Mabs had told her, instead took out the dark-blue blanket beneath which she had slept the previous night – a blanket much too small for her, and printed all over with silver stars. Looking at it now, she knew the blanket must have been Daisy's. Daisy had stars on everything – her tent, her toys, her bedclothes. And it must have been important to Fay, for her to have taken it on her run. How could she have forgotten it? And yet, somehow, she clearly had. Could this be Alberon's doing?

She thought back to the previous night. It seemed so long ago to her now, so far away, in another world. But she remembered dancing with him, and sharing a madcap cigarette, and drinking a cup of that harsh, but somehow smoky, woodland spirit—

I accepted his hospitality, thought Fay to herself in dismay. *That's why I forgot Daisy's blanket.* How many of her memories had she already lost to him? And what unknown risks was she taking, just by being in his kingdom?

She spread Daisy's blanket on the gleaming granite floor. It was cold and hard, but the layer of fabric would give her some protection. Her running things were gone, and only the hoodie in her backpack and the dress made by the tailor bees remained. She put the dress on, and the hoodie for warmth, and lay on the blanket on the ground, using her pack as a pillow. She did not expect to be comfortable: and so it was with some surprise that she awoke from a dark and dreamless sleep to find herself on a railway platform, deserted, with no sign of life, and saw it was morning.

The Night Train

≈

Dan he took out his pipes to play,
Bit sair his hert wi d'ol an wae.

Child Ballad no. 19: *King Orfeo*

One

For a moment, she was disoriented. Where was the beautiful chamber? The bath, with its feet of polished brass? The four-poster bed, like a sailing ship? The clusters of blinking torchflies?

All that was gone. The bedchamber had become a railway station. High above her head, a glass roof allowed a cold and wintry light to filter onto the platform. The gleaming granite floor had changed to a worn and grubby concrete. The dress that she had worn to the ball had become a scant thing of colourless rags that disintegrated like cobwebs at the touch of her fingers. Her running shoes were still intact, except for the missing laces, but otherwise she was wearing nothing but her underthings and the oversized hoodie, which had belonged to Allan, and thus was large enough to pass as some kind of minidress.

She rolled up Daisy's blanket and looked around. Where was she now? What world was this? The station was not unlike King's Cross, but without any of the chaos of London Beyond, or the dark brilliance of London Beneath. A pale dust lay on everything, undisturbed but for the marks of her presence. Could this be Nethermost London? And if so, where was the Night Train?

Looking across the railway lines, Fay could see no sign of a train. The signal at the platform's end gleamed a dark, impassive red. There were no departure boards; no advertisements; no graffiti. A single bench stood on the platform, although there was no sign of other passengers. She could not even be certain that the pale light above her was daylight. She looked for her shadow on the ground. It seemed rather fainter than usual, though whether this was due to the muted light or Alberon's glamours, she could not tell. She realized she was hungry but searching through her backpack she found only the crumbs from her cereal bar and a mouthful of water left in the bottle. There were no vending machines in the station, and no sign of shops, or an exit; and so Fay finished her crumbs and drank the dregs of her water, and bundled

Daisy's blanket away, and tried to fix the broken straps of her backpack by knotting them firmly together, and then she sat down on the bench and tried to list all the details she could about her life in London, to see if she could identify any gaps in her memory. But all that seemed very far away; far away and long ago, and all she could really be sure of was the glimpse she had seen of Daisy that night, through the crack in the pavement—

Then she remembered the notebook that was clipped to her key ring. She searched for her keys and located the book, no larger than a matchbox, with its tiny pencil attached. It was far from easy to use: her fingers were clumsy, the pencil so small, and yet she managed to use it to write, in words almost too small to read:

Daisy's eyes: blue. Her hair: brown. Favourite toy: her stuffed tiger.

Fay frowned, trying to recall the name of the tiger. Had it even *had* a name? She remembered the little travelling girl saying to her in London Below: *Tigers don't have names*. Had Daisy said that too? Fay couldn't remember. The girl *had* looked like Daisy, she thought: perhaps she had confused the memories.

123

Or maybe it didn't happen, said a quiet voice at the back of her mind. *Maybe you were dreaming, and none of this ever happened at all.*

'That isn't true,' said Fay, as if someone had spoken the words aloud. Perhaps they had; she told herself. Perhaps this was another of Alberon's tricks, and she was still in London Beneath, asleep on the gold-studded granite floor.

If you say so, said the voice, and once more Fay turned around to make sure no one had spoken. *But tell me, how did Daisy die? Tell me again. I've forgotten.*

Fay shook her head. 'I don't have to,' she said.

She stepped in front of a train, didn't she? said the voice relentlessly. *Stepped under a speeding train that didn't stop at the station?* Fay said nothing. The voice went on: *Do you think perhaps this obsession with trains might have something to do with that?*

Fay shook her head. 'You're not real,' she said.

As opposed to the giant moths, and talking tigers? Oh, Fay, said the voice, and now Fay thought that perhaps she knew whose voice it was. Janine, her therapist, had precisely the same tone of slightly jaded sympathy. *Don't you think it's more likely that you've had some kind of an incident? Maybe you were mugged, Fay, on your nightly run through the West End. Or maybe you're inventing all this as a diversion from the truth: that you'll never see your daughter again?*

Once more, Fay shook her head. 'That isn't true,' she said aloud.

Oh, but it is, said the quiet voice. *And now you're sitting half-naked on a railway platform, talking to people who aren't there, waiting for a train that will never come.*

'Be quiet! This isn't a dream!' cried Fay. Her voice clanged against the brickwork of the empty station. But there was less conviction in it, and at the back of her mind there was a cold and growing fear that if she stopped and listened hard, she might hear the sounds of the *real* King's Cross ringing out between the Worlds…

'It wasn't a dream,' she repeated. 'It wasn't a dream. I can prove it.' And from the pocket of her pack she brought out the rose that had come to her on the wind of London Beyond: its petals slightly withered now, but red as the heart of a furnace.

A rose? said the inner voice mockingly.

'The rose that came to me *after* I saw Daisy through the pavement cracks,' Fay said with a surge of triumph. '*After* I met Alberon. *After* I woke up on the street.'

Proving nothing, said the voice, although it lacked conviction.

But Fay had regained her self-confidence. Picking up the pencil once more, she wrote in the tiny note-book:

The cake I made when she was four, shaped like Thomas the Tank Engine.
The first time she went to the theatre.
The sandcastle we built, the three of us, on the beach in Brighton.
The coffee shop at King's Cross, with a cup of chocolate.
Feeding the squirrels in Green Park.
The toy theatre Allan made for her third birthday.
Her first day at school.
Her first Christmas.
Her blue tent, embroidered with stars.
In the park on Bonfire Night, writing our names with a sparkler.
Making cookies with Allan and me.
The pavement game.
The Shadowless Man.
Grabbing my finger, the day she was born. It felt as if she would never let go.

And then with a final effort, she wrote:

I'll never forget her. Whatever it costs. I saw her, asleep in the bluebells. I'll find her, and I'll bring her back. My plaid shall not be blown away.

At the back of her mind, the inner voice gave a kind of defeated sigh. Fay smiled and kept on writing. These stories had power. She knew that now. She found herself singing as she wrote:

> *My plaid away, my plaid away,*
> *My plaid shall not be blown away.*

TWO

Time passes at a different pace in the path of the river Dream. Fay tried to work out how long she had been waiting on the platform, but her phone had run out of battery, and her Fitbit was telling her that it was six in the morning, midnight and ten minutes past five on 8 April, 3 June and 19 December simultaneously.

She put the Fitbit into her pack, next to the blanket and the dead phone. The light from the station roof had not changed since she had woken up, and there was no way of telling if it was daylight up there, or some other form of illumination. *When will the train arrive?* she thought. *How will I get on board?* She had no money to speak of: besides, she guessed that her currency would have no value in this world. So what did she have to offer? *Tales and songs are his currency,*

Mabs had told her in London Beneath. Well, Fay knew plenty of both, she thought, but what kind of story would summon the Train? Once more she thought of the travelling girl; the tiger; Alberon and his people. All had shared versions of that same song – a song that told the mysterious tale of a knight whose horn could summon the winds...

> *The elphin knight sits on yon hill,*
> *Bay, bay, lily, bay.*
> *He blows his horn both loud and shrill,*
> *The wind hath blown my plaid away.*
>
> *My plaid away, my plaid away,*
> *And o'er the hill and far away,*
> *And o'er the sea to Norroway,*
> *My plaid shall not be blown away.*

Her voice was a little uncertain, but it rang across the platform. And couldn't she feel a distant response – a subtle resonance – that gilded the air like pollen and lifted the fine hairs on her arms?

Fay stood up and looked at the red-light signal. It showed no sign of changing: it shone as bright as the sun on a winter rose. What kind of stories had Mabs meant? Was this another riddle?

For a moment her mind went back to the tale of King Orfeo and the Oracle. The King had rescued his wife, and yet, robbed of her shadow, she had been unable to remember her life, or rekindle her love for him. Like the knight in the song, the Oracle had given the King three riddles to solve before he and his wife could be together again.

When you can make me a cambric shirt...
Without any seam or needlework—

There must be a solution, she knew. But a shirt without seams or needlework? Even allowing for poetic licence, how was that possible?

Just then, Fay noticed something perched on the flap of her backpack. Looking closer, she saw that it was one of the tailor bees that had helped weave her gown the previous night. It was alive, but barely: for the air of Nethermost London was cold, and there were no flowers to be seen anywhere in the station.

Fay held the tiny bee in the palm of her hand. It looked so out of place in this world. She wished she could help it, somehow. And then she thought of the red rose, and taking it out of her backpack again, she set the tailor bee down gently onto the scarlet petals. Maybe it would find nourishment there. The bee crawled into the heart of the rose and Fay heard it begin to buzz contentedly. She gently replaced the rose and the bee into the pack's side pocket.

And then she realized that she knew the first part of the riddle. 'The answer is bees,' she said aloud. 'The first part of the riddle is bees.'

Fay looked at the signal-light again. The light had dimmed, she was certain of it. Her head felt suddenly as light as after a dose of madcap. At the time she'd assumed it was the madcap smoke that had shown her the vision of Daisy, but could it have been the *song itself* that had opened the crack in the pavement?

The signal light was definitely a little dimmer than before. Fay searched in her mind for the words of the song, fearing she had forgotten them, but there they were, and the melody too, as clear as a childhood memory. She stepped up to the platform edge, clutching her pack like a lost child, and raising her voice, she let it rise like a cloud of butterflies:

> *My plaid away, my plaid away*
> *And o'er the hill and far away…*

The signal was visibly darkening, changing slowly from red to green, and now Fay could hear a roaring sound, like an approaching hurricane, like a tide of floodwater running along the railway tracks, like a swarm of wild bees, although there was still no train in sight—

She raised her voice, feeling it soar, sweet and powerful and strong:

And o'er the sea to Norroway…

Now she could feel the slipstream dragging at her hair, her clothes, but still there was no train in sight, and no change but for the signal light that now shone green as springtime. *The easiest way to board the Night Train is to die*, she thought. What if all this was a mistake? What if the inner voice was right, and the Night Train would not accept her fare?

She took a breath. The air was sweet as honeycomb.

'My plaid shall not be blown away,' she said firmly and, closing her eyes, her pack still held tightly against her body, she stepped right off the station platform and into the path of the Night Train.

Three

For a moment Fay was in darkness. Her head was filled with tumbling stars; her heart raced like an engine. Then she opened her eyes to find herself lying on a carpeted floor, a floor that thrummed and shuddered.

For a few terrifying seconds, Fay had no idea where she was. What was she doing? What was this place? Then her outstretched hand touched her pack, and her memory returned. She was on another train, she saw: a train that seemed to be travelling through a tunnel – the stutter of lights through the windows was the only illumination.

She struggled to her feet, keeping hold of her backpack as she did so. Now she remembered the travelling girl; the station and the Night Train. She remembered Mabs and Alberon, and the hellride into London Beneath, and waking up on the platform at last, dressed in nothing but spider silk and her dead husband's hoodie. A light came on in the carriage now; it was yellow and intermittent, but it gave her the chance to look around and take in her surroundings. The seats were of ancient velvet, the carriage windows milky with age. And in the seats were passengers, looking wanly through the glass, their dead and expressionless faces livid in the corpse-light.

'Excuse me?' said Fay.

No one replied. Her fellow travellers sat and stared, unblinking, through the windows.

'Is there anyone in charge?' called Fay, but her voice sounded dead and exhausted in the velvet-lined interior. She found a vacant seat and sat down. From outside came a blur of light as the train flashed through a station. Fay read a sign on the white tile wall: ELPHAME. And then they were back in the hurtling dark, and she watched the tunnel lights strobing. Sometimes she caught glimpses of their surroundings, flashing by at the speed of Dream. Sometimes they seemed to be underground, sometimes high above the clouds; sometimes running through desert sands, sometimes underwater. And the signs flashing by said: TIR NA NOG, THE LAND OF ROAST

BEEF, or FAERIE, or ALFHEIM, or XANADU, or ATLANTIS. But however intently she looked, she saw nothing that looked like the place she had seen through the cracks in the pavement; and even if she did, she thought, how would she stop the train?

She turned to the nearest passenger, a woman in her twenties, wearing jeans and a pink sleeveless top and a vinyl necklace. In another kind of light she might have been pretty, but in the intermittent gleam of the Night Train's exhausted cells, she looked as dead as the rest of them. Fay put out a hand to touch her bare arm. The young woman did not respond.

'Talk to me. Please. Am I still alive? Is this the Night Train?'

Still the woman said nothing.

Fay reached out to touch the woman's necklace. The name MAISIE had been laser-cut out of a piece of black vinyl, and studded with little crystal stars. 'Maisie? Is that your name?' she said. 'Maisie, please. Talk to me.'

At the sound of her name, the young woman's eyes finally quickened into a kind of awareness. She turned her head slightly, parted her lips and whispered:

'A named thing is a tamed thing. I speak as I must, and cannot lie.'

Fay's heart gave a leap, and she took the young

woman's hand in hers. 'How do I find the Hallowe'en King? Where do I ask the Night Train to stop?'

Maisie gave a weary sigh. 'The Night Train never stops,' she said. 'I speak as I must, and cannot lie.'

'But it *has* to stop!' said Fay. 'The Hallowe'en King has my daughter.'

'The Hallowe'en King takes his due. I speak as I must, and cannot lie.'

Fay struggled with the urge to cry from sheer frustration and fatigue. But she had not come so far simply to give up now. 'The Train *will* stop for me,' she said. 'All I need to know is where.'

Maisie sighed again, and said: 'Dream is a river that runs to the sea. I speak as I must, and—'

'So tell me!' said Fay. 'How do I get to the Hallowe'en King? How do I make him give Daisy back?'

Maisie gave a final sigh. Her voice, faint from the start, had grown almost inaudible. *'If you can find me an acre of land between the salt water and the sea sand,'* she whispered, her eyes beginning to close. 'Then, and only then...' Her whispering voice fell silent once more. The fleeting life in her features was gone. And Fay was alone on the Night Train, with only the dead for company.

Four

For a time, Fay travelled in silence, looking out at the scenery. Sometimes they travelled in darkness: sometimes through a field of stars; sometimes underwater or across bright meadows of sunflowers. The stations were places from legend and dream; cities long vanished; deserts unknown. Some had names that she recognized; others were written in foreign script, hieroglyphics or ancient runes.

Inside the carriage, nothing moved. The passengers – even Maisie – were impossible to rouse. Fay wondered how she had managed to communicate with the young woman at all. Perhaps only because she had known her name – after all, hadn't Maisie said: *A named thing is a tamed thing?*

Was that another riddle? It had not escaped Fay's

notice that Maisie's reply to her last question had been very like the riddle the Oracle had given King Orfeo. And the words with which she punctuated each answer was similar, too: *I speak as I must, and cannot lie.* It could hardly be by chance: that story, thought Fay, was linked to hers in ways that could not be coincidental. Bees had been the first clue, and Fay had managed to solve it, and buy her passage on the Night Train. But… a land between the shore and the sea? A man without a shadow? Surely these were simply ways of asking the impossible?

And yet a riddle had brought her on board. Perhaps another could direct her where she needed to go? And so she raised her voice and sang to her audience of the dead:

> *Who can find me an acre of land,*
> *Bay, bay, lily, bay*
> *Between the salt water and the sea sand?*
> *The wind hath blown my plaid away.*

For a time nothing happened. Fay's voice sounded strange and flat inside the crowded carriage. But then she began to become aware of a change in the sound of the engines; a slowing of the scenes outside as they passed through the alien countryside. Until finally, in

a long squeal of brakes, the Night Train stopped at
a platform by the side of a long grey beach, with no
sign of habitation but a hand-lettered sign that read:
NORROWA.

Norrowa

≈

'I have an aiker of good ley-land,
Which lyeth low by yon sea-
strand.'

Child Ballad no. 2:
The Elphin Knight

One

Fay stepped out onto the platform, still carrying her backpack. The air was mild and smelt of the sea, and of the salt of the sandy dunes that lined the deserted platform. There was no sign of any kind of human habitation: no road; no buildings; nothing but the dunes, and the path to the beach, and beyond it, the gleaming grey ocean. A few blue thistles lined the boards; otherwise, the platform was bare. Fay took off her running shoes and stepped barefoot onto the sandy path. She turned – and saw that during those moments, the platform, the rails, the hand-lettered sign and the Night Train itself had all vanished, leaving nothing but dune and grass, and the long, bare, bleak expanse of the beach, shining in the sunlight. The shadows were long, the sun low, and there was nothing to hear but the keening sound of the wind and the waves on the sand. Where was she? Her head felt strangely light, and looking for her shadow, she saw that it was unusually faint against the mica-speckled sand.

A phrase from a song came back to her: *The wind hath blown my plaid away.* What was the song? The memory seemed very distant, and yet it felt somehow significant. She closed her eyes and tried to recall why it had been so important to leave the train. What had she been looking for? She looked down at her backpack and for a moment could not recall who it belonged to, or where it was from: then she saw the corner of Daisy's blanket poking out from under the flap, and remembered why her shadow was dim –

I accepted a ride on the Night Train. I forced one of the dead to speak. And I accepted the challenge that Lord Death gave to King Orfeo.

Fay's heart seemed to tighten with dread. How much of her memory had she lost? She opened the backpack and laid out the contents onto the sand. The blanket of stars; the tailor bee; the rose; her phone, the first-aid kit and the key ring, with the tiny notebook attached. She opened the book and read aloud the words she had written the night before, but none of them seemed like memories. She still remembered

Daisy, of course, and the terrible grief of losing her, but the memories she had written down – the sand-castle, the birthday cake – seemed as remote as the Night Train now, with all its silent passengers. There was no recognition, no spark: no light behind the images. She thought of a Polaroid photograph, fading out of existence. That was all that remained of them now. The words were only a story.

She picked up the tiny pencil and wrote:

I am still losing my memories. Payment for the progress I've made. Mabs warned me to keep my plaid close. I have to remember Daisy.

And then she wrote:

Daisy's princess dress, all white, embroidered with silver stars. She wanted to wear it all the time. With a sword, of course: because why shouldn't princesses have swords?
A cherry strudel, on a bench, at a Christmas market.
The first time she went on an aeroplane, and how she said she could see the clouds from the top of the sky.
The answer to the first was bees. I'm here to find the second.

There were now only two tiny pages left of the little notebook.

Fay slipped it into her pocket and turned towards the ocean, which shone like a shield in the burnished sunlight. The sea was going out: she could see the gleaming of the wet sand. A cone-shaped shell lay on the shore, larger than any she had ever seen.

He blows his horn both loud and shrill, thought Fay, and picked up the seashell. It felt smooth and inviting.

I wonder, would it make a sound? Fay raised it to her lips. There was a tiny aperture at the sharp end of the shell, and blowing into it, she thought she heard whalesong, low and sweet and melancholy, over the sound of the waves on the beach.

The sun was setting at her back, sending the shadows sprawling. Even her own, faint as it was, stretched all the way to the tideline. She put the seashell in her pack, along with the rose and the blanket of stars. *Over the sea to Norroway*, she thought, as she stood on the seashore, watching the silver sky darken to blue, until at last all the shadows were gone, and nothing was left but a river of stars.

Two

Fay lay on her back on the sand with her pack as a pillow. The stars were coldly, achingly bright, wrapping the night in a broad, bright band. Slowly the moon rose over the sea, painting a silver path to the shore. Then came the bats – hundreds of them, swooping and dancing like butterflies across the broken face of the moon. They reminded Fay of Alberon, and of how he and Moth and Peronelle had vanished into a cloud of wings. She remembered that night vividly: the moonlit statue of Anteros; the madcap and the butterflies; the vision of Daisy through the cracks. Whatever had happened to her mind and to her memories of home, *these* memories were still intact, like the tale of King Orfeo, and the Oracle's riddle:

Who can find me an acre of land,
Between the salt water and the sea sand?

The words had power. The riddle, too. And had not the tiger told her there was truth to be found in stories? Alberon's tale of the Queen who left her kingdom to fall in love; the tale of King Orfeo and the Hallowe'en King; the Oracle's mocking answer – all these were linked to some deeper truth, some message she was meant to decode. And under the glamours and stories and tricks, through the veil of the madcap smoke and her failing memory, she knew that Daisy was waiting. She had to solve the second part of the riddle. The Night Train had carried her thus far – surely for a reason. And so she lay on the cool dark sand and watched the river of stars above, and listened to the sound of the waves that slowly crept back up the beach, and somewhere between the tideline and the pale rags of the rising waves, Fay heard the sound of distant song, and soon fell asleep and was dreaming.

Three

Dream is a river that runs to the sea, the dead girl on the train had said. And now Fay dreamed – or *thought* she dreamed – of lying on the beach at night, looking up at the circling stars, with the sound of the sea all around her. The moon was high now, pale and sharp above a silver bank of cloud: its light shone on the water like a ladder to the sky. And in her dream Fay saw a ship moored between the banks of cloud; a ship that shone with the light of the stars, its sails as fine as spider silk, and she could see people clinging to the rigging and looking down from the deck, and soaring like birds around the hull on wings that gleamed like moonlight.

Awake or asleep, Fay thought it was the most beautiful thing she had ever seen; and as she watched, she realized that she could hear voices, raised in song above the rushing of the sea:

> *There lived a king unto the east*
> *(Blow, blow, the winds blow)*
> *Who loved a queen unto the west*
> *(Green, green, the hedgerow).*
>
> *The king he has a-hunting gone*
> *(Blow, blow, the winds blow)*
> *And left his true love all alone*
> *(Green, green, the hedgerow).*
>
> *The King o' Faërie, with his dart,*
> *(Blow, blow, the winds blow)*
> *Hath pierced the lady to the heart*
> *(Green, green, the hedgerow).*
>
> *Hath kept her in his fortress deep*
> *(Blow, blow, the winds blow)*
> *Within the realm of endless sleep*
> *(Green, green, the hedgerow).*
>
> *But King Orfeo in pursuit*
> *(Blow, blow, the winds blow)*
> *Played a reel upon his flute*
> *(Green, green, the hedgerow).*

And first he played the notes of noy
(Blow, blow, the winds blow)
And then he played the notes of joy
(Green, green, the hedgerow).

And then he played the gabber reel
(Blow, blow, the winds blow)
The notes that make a sick heart hale
(Green, green, the hedgerow).

'What does it mean?' said Fay aloud. The song had sounded so familiar, the words so intimate and strange. There had to be a message in there – it could be no coincidence that this was a version of Alberon's tale of King Orfeo and the Hallowe'en King, who, in this version, seemed to be the King of Faërie. She thought of the travelling girl's words in London Beyond: *Some call him Lord Death, the Harlequin, the Erl-King, or the Elphin Knight. Sometimes they call him the Shadowless Man.*

The Shadowless Man. The object of Daisy's night terrors featured in the story that had brought her here. A man of many identities; a trickster and a teller of tales, who could, depending on the circumstance, be either the King of Faërie or the Lord of the Kingdom of Death.

Stories and songs are his currency, Mabs had told her.

Riddles too. She had been speaking of Alberon. But in this version of the Orpheus tale, Hades and Oberon seemed to be interchangeable. Of course, it was only a dream, she thought, looking up into the brilliant sky. The sky-ship was still sailing there, sails unfurled like Northern Lights. And yet she could feel the sand beneath her palms, smell the sharp scent of the surf, feel the chill of the sea wind against her bare legs. It all felt so real. Was she dreaming at all?

Dream is a river that runs to the sea, the dead girl on the train had said. And if Mabs were to be believed, the Night Train itself was powered by dreams and riddles and ballads and stories. *Over the sea to Norroway*, she thought, and felt the hairs on her arms rise as if in response to the words.

Once more she looked up at the sky-ship, gleaming in the moonlit sky. Then she closed her eyes and thought once more of the Oracle's riddle:

> *Who can find me an acre of land,*
> *Between the salt water and the sea sand?*

'The answer is Dream,' she said aloud. 'The second part of the riddle is Dream.'

And then she opened her eyes to find it was daylight once more, and that she was standing on the bank of a broad and fast-running river, while far beyond, in the distance, stretched a bone-grey, bone-dry expanse of sand. The sky was grey; the ground was grey, but the river – if it *was* a river – seemed made up of shining fragments like pieces of tinsel, or fireflies, or flares of incandescent gas. And up, behind and over her there loomed a shadow dark as Death, which, when she turned to look at it, revealed itself to be a cliff so high that it vanished into the clouds.

'Those are the cliffs of Damnation,' said a voice at Fay's side. 'And on the far side of the river Dream is the Kingdom of the Dead.'

Four

Fay turned, and saw a young woman standing beside her on the bank. Her hair was closely cropped, and her eyes were dark and sweet as honeycomb. She was wearing ripped jeans and a T-shirt printed with the words: LONG AGO AND FAR AWAY. She looked vaguely familiar, though Fay could not quite place her. And in one hand she held the rose that Fay had found on Euston road, as long ago and far away as anything from a fairy tale.

'Who are you?' said Fay.

The young woman smiled. 'I am many things. A woman of the travelling folk. A tailor bee. An old friend. Today I am a messenger, here to deliver a warning.' She held up the rose to inhale its scent. The flower was slightly faded now, but the scent was still surprisingly strong, filling the dead air with sweetness. 'Nothing is scented here,' she said. 'Nothing beautiful grows here. This is the Shadowless Land, a province of the Kingdom of Death. And only by leaving your shadow behind can you hope to find your daughter again.'

'My shadow?'

The young woman nodded.

'But wouldn't I also lose the memory of my former life?'

The young woman shrugged. 'Lord Death takes his toll. His rules date back to the birth of the Worlds, and memory cannot linger in the Shadowless Land, where Life is nothing but a dream, and even Love is forgotten.'

'I could never forget Daisy,' said Fay.

'Then take your chance,' said the young woman serenely.

Fay thought back to the tale of King Orfeo and the Oracle. *'To free your lady,' the Oracle said, 'you must find the madcap mushroom, which grows in the caves on the shores of Dream, under the cliffs of Damnation.'*

She turned once more to the dark-eyed woman. 'To pass into the Kingdom of Death, I need the madcap mushroom,' she said. 'Can you show me where it grows?'

'I can show you,' the young woman said. 'But to use it here is dangerous. It gives the taker the power to pass through the islands of Dream at will. But Dream is a dangerous country, my Queen. You will need all your courage and strength to cross it with your mind intact.'

'And yet I must,' said Fay, 'if I am to reach the Hallowe'en King and ask him to free my daughter.'

The young woman said, 'Very well, my Queen. I will show you the madcap mushroom, which grows in the caves deep under the cliffs. This I will do, in return for my life, which you saved in Nethermost London. But I cannot help you in Dream. There you will either cross over, or drown.'

And with those words she led Fay into the shadow that lay at the foot of the cliff that reached above them into the clouds. For a moment the darkness was so complete that Fay had to feel her way along the rough, dank walls of the passageway. But little by little, as they advanced, her vision began to adjust, and she saw that she was in a cave that was broader and higher than any Fay had ever seen or imagined. There was a lake in the distance, lit by dim phosphorescence, and in the nooks and cracks in the wall there grew small five-petalled flowers that looked like strawberry blossoms and gave off a sweet and earthy scent.

'No, not those, my Queen,' said her guide, as Fay stopped to smell the flowers. 'Here is the madcap mushroom, that led King Orfeo into the Lands of Death, and which, if used correctly, will take you to the Hallowe'en King.'

She indicated a fungus that was growing out from the side of the wall. 'A single dose,' she said, 'will take you into the realms of Dream. But whatever you see there, keep moving. The bubble-worlds and skerries of Dream are not for you to inhabit. And if you reach the Lord of Death, take nothing, not even a handshake from him, for if you do, you and your Daisy will stay in his kingdom for ever.'

And at that the young woman's image dissolved into a golden blur of bees that fanned out over the shining lake like a plume of dragonfire.

'Wait!' called Fay. 'How much is a dose? What is the answer to the final riddle? And' – her voice echoed forlornly around the enormous cavern –'tell me, how did King Orfeo come to lose his shadow?'

But there was no answer from the young woman who had guided her, except for the distant drone of bees, far away, in the darkness.

Five

Her feet were sore. Fay realized that she had left her shoes on the beach. She was feeling cold, too, so she took Daisy's blanket from her pack, and tied it, sarong-style, around her waist. The madcap mushroom that grew from the wall gave off a faint and pallid glow. *Correctly used* – what did that mean? Was she supposed to smoke the thing, or swallow it? She didn't know. And what would happen if she were to use it *in*correctly?

There's no time for this, she thought. *I'm so close to reaching Daisy.* The mushroom might be poison, or she might use it incorrectly, but she couldn't know until she tried. And so she broke off one of the thin pale stems of the fungus growing out of the wall, brought it close to her face, and inhaled the scent of the madcap mushroom.

A bitter luminescence drooled out of the broken part of the stem, and a scent of something muddled and sweet – and by now, very familiar – filled the air of the cavern. It was the scent of the madcap smoke, but oily, and less volatile: the scent of something that has grown for far too long away from the sun. It made her remember how long it was since she had eaten or drunk anything. But there was nothing to be done about that until she was back in her own world – for had not the tailor bee warned her? And so she inhaled the madcap scent, and tried not to think of anything, and felt the world blossom around her, turning the dark of the cavern into an astonishing plume of sounds and scents and colours.

'My plaid shall not be blown away,' said Fay to herself. The meaning of the mysterious phrase might have been unclear to her, but its power was unmistakable, for the colours responded to the words, making spirals in the dark, which beckoned to her eagerly. Well, for want of a plaid, Fay thought, she could at least keep her blanket close, and wrapping it tighter about her waist, she clutched her backpack to her chest and prepared to face the onslaught of Dream.

The Hallowe'en King

≈

An first he played da notes o noy,
An dan he played da notes o joy.
An dan he played da g'od gabber reel,
Dat meicht ha made a sick herl hale.

Child Ballad no. 19: *King Orfeo*

One

It came to her first as memory. *Memory is a bubble*, thought Fay, *in a river made of Time*, and the river Dream took hold of that thought and shaped it into a tiny world that spun and sparkled like a bauble on a Christmas tree—

That Christmas, thought Fay. *Our first one together, the three of us, when Daisy was only eight months old. Allan brought the Christmas tree home, and we hung the baubles all over it – glass baubles that were silver and scarlet and gold, and sparkled like all the worlds of Dream...*

For a second, Fay could actually see herself inside the bauble. And then she was *there* – in London, at home, with Allan sitting beside the tree and Daisy beside him, on the floor, among the wrapping paper.

Allan was wearing a red checked shirt, a Christmas

163

present from Fay that year, and Fay a white cashmere jumper. Daisy was in her pink sleepsuit, her stuffed tiger under one arm. And the scent was cut pine and cinnamon, and orange peel and nutmeg and clove, and Fay knew without looking that there would be Christmas cake in the kitchen, and apples baked in spices, and mince pies dusted with sugar, and wine mulled with sugar and allspice. She knew that night would bring them stars, and a new moon and a sparkling frost, and stifled laughter, and long slow love, and a feeling that this could never end…

'It never has to,' Allan said, looking at her and smiling.

His voice was warm and familiar, his presence impossibly real and strong. 'No, no, this is a dream,' she said. 'I have to find Daisy.'

'Daisy's right here,' Allan said. 'Everything you want is here. Dream is a river that runs through every world there is, or was, or can be imagined. And Dream has brought you back to me. Wouldn't you rather stay here?'

'Oh, Allan,' said Fay. She *did* want to stay – to be here at a time when things were safe and good, and they were a family – but how long does a dream last? Fifteen seconds? A minute? More? Already the colours were fading; the plaid of Allan's shirt had changed from bright red-and-black to a dusty rose. Daisy's eyes were on her now (*Her eyes were blue. Remember that*, thought Fay to herself), looking wide and anxious. *This is for Daisy*, she told herself. *This is to bring Daisy home.*

'Allan, I can't. I love you, but—'

'Please, Fay, don't forget me,' he said. 'The thoughts of the living are all the dead can hope for. Memory keeps us alive. Let it go, and I may as well never have existed at all.'

'I'm sorry, darling. I have to—'

'Don't go. Just take my hand and stay with me. Here, where no one can reach us.' He stretched out his hand and smiled at her. 'Don't be afraid. Just take my hand. We can be together for ever.'

This isn't fair! Fay thought. *Why did no one tell me Dream would be so cruel?*

She closed her eyes and clenched her fists in the fabric of Daisy's blanket. *What made you think it would be fair?* said a dry voice in her mind. *Is Life fair? Is Death fair? So why should Dream be different?*

The voice was vaguely familiar, although she could not place it. Was it a voice from Norroway? The Night Train? Nethermost London? In any case, it spoke the truth from deep within her memory. *To get your Daisy back*, it said, *you must give as well as take: and when you have given all you can, then maybe you can earn your reward...*

Allan was watching her, hand outstretched. His eyes, so kind and familiar, were dark with pain and foreknowledge. 'You're going to forget me,' he said. 'You may not mean to, but you will. This memory, and so much more, will be lost like a soap-bubble in the sun. And when you set foot on the shore of Death, you will have nothing left to pay your debt to the Hallowe'en King.'

'Pay him what? What debt?' said Fay.

'The price of Daisy's life, of course. *When you can walk shadowless at noon...*' They were the words of the Oracle: the last part of the riddle.

'Do you know the answer?' she said. 'Please, Allan, I have to know.'

Allan sighed. His face had become as insubstantial as morning mist. 'I speak as I must, my love,' he said. 'I speak as I must, and cannot say more.' And then, both he and the dream were gone, and Fay found herself on a sandy shore, with tears on her face, and no memory of why she had been weeping.

Two

The sun was shining. The sky was blue as only memories can be. Fay felt a warm well-being in every part of her body. The sand was warm under her feet, and she realized that she was barefoot, and wearing a blanket around her waist. She had a backpack with her, too; a broken, ragged scrap of a thing, empty but for a large, cone-shaped seashell.

The blanket was old and faded. The pack was missing both its straps. And yet there was something that stopped her from simply leaving them behind. She put a hand into her pocket, and found a key ring, on which hung a tiny notebook. Opening the notebook, she saw that on the penultimate page someone had scrawled the mysterious phrase: *My plaid has not been blown away.*

I'm supposed to remember what that means, thought Fay. *Why can't I remember?*

There was a little girl on the beach, building a castle in the sand. She must have been about six years old, blonde, and wearing a yellow dress. Her eyes were blue and filled with stars. *Your name is Daisy Orr*, thought Fay. *You're Daisy, and I love you.*

She went over to the little girl and sat down on the hot white sand. Daisy looked up and smiled. 'I made a moat for my castle,' she said. 'Now we just wait for the sea to come in.' And then the child began to sing a song Fay almost recognized:

> *My father left me three acres of land,*
> *Parsley, sage, rosemary and thyme—*

Those aren't the words, said Fay to herself. And yet, it was the very same song she had used to board the Night Train; to cross the sea to Norroway; to reach the shore of Dream – and now she remembered those things again, like pictures from another life. She remembered the rose, and the madcap smoke, the tailor bees, and Alberon; and, looking down at the hot white sand, she saw what was left of her shadow, fainter than a heat haze.

For a moment all she could feel was dismay. So

much of her memory was gone. But the vision of Daisy, asleep, through the cracks in the pavement below Piccadilly was clear, and she knew what she was here to do. *The first of the Oracle's riddles was bees, the second Dream, and the third, the third...*

'Your father,' said Fay. 'I loved him so much. And yet I don't remember him.' The thought filled her with a sudden grief. Was this the price of her journey so far? And when would her debt be paid in full?

'He's gone,' said the child. 'He fell through the cracks between the Worlds, and the Shadowless Man took him away. But *you'll* stay, won't you? *You* won't leave me?'

'Oh, sweetheart,' said Fay. 'Of course I won't. I came all this way to find you.'

'Then stay with me,' said Daisy. 'Stay until the sea comes in, and my castle is all washed away. We'll lie on the beach and watch the stars and be here, together, for ever and ever.'

But now Fay could see the sides of the dream, like a soap-bubble ready to burst. The sky was several shades lighter already; the sea had lost its rich dark shine. The sun was veiled, and on the sand, there was no longer any trace of her shadow. She held out her arms and Daisy crept into their sheltering circle, but already she felt insubstantial, her body an armful of butterflies, ready to scatter to the winds.

When I leave this dream, thought Fay, *will this memory be gone? Daisy, aged six, in her yellow dress, building a sandcastle on the beach?* She feared that it would: and yet she knew this was the only way to reach the other side of Dream, where the Hallowe'en King was waiting.

The dream world was losing substance fast: Fay closed her eyes and tried to hold onto the image of her daughter's face as it faded from her memory. *Daisy's eyes were blue*, she thought. *Her eyes were blue. Remember that.* And then she raised her voice and sang the last of the Oracle's riddles:

> *When you can walk shadowless at noon*
> *Every sage grows merry in time…*

And opened her eyes on the dusty, desert, sunless shore of Death – which, of course, was the answer.

Three

The first was Bees.

The second was Dream.

The third was Death.

And Death was all around her. It was in the strange, pale sky; the dusty ground; the thousand tiny fragments that shone like mica in the air. *So this is Death. It isn't so bad*, Fay thought as she scanned the horizon. Death's country is all absences; absence of scent; absence of sound; absence of the sun in the sky. No shadow on the hard, dry sand. No heat; no cold; no pain; no regret; nothing but her consciousness standing on the shore of Dream, with a handful of star-patterned rags, a notebook and a seashell –

This must have been something important, she thought, looking at the ragged remains of the blanket tied around her waist. *I brought it here for a reason. Why?* But try as she might, she could not recall and, seeing it so faded and torn, she let it fall to the dusty ground, where the wind-blown sands were gathering. Next, she placed the seashell into the pouch of her hoodie and opened the tiny notebook. Maybe it would remind her of what she had forgotten.

She read the words: *I'll never forget her. Whatever it costs. I saw her, asleep in the bluebells.* And with that came the memory of looking through a crack in the ground, and seeing a girl, asleep in the woods—

Daisy, thought Fay. *My Daisy. Her eyes were blue, and I loved her.* And once more, she remembered why she was there, and raising her voice to the hard grey sky, she said in a voice that rang across the desert like a summons:

'The first was bees. The second was Dream. The third was Death. Now come to me; I will sing you a song the like of which you have never heard, and you will give me my daughter back, and then my tale will be told.'

For a time there was no reply from the dusty plains of Death. And then Fay heard the sound of laughter behind her, and turned to see a man standing there on the turbulent shore of Dream. A man – she could not in fairness say if he was a friend or a stranger –

his face, his handsome profile both well known and unfamiliar. His hair was dark and shoulder-length; a gemstone gleamed on one pale hand.

Had she met him before? Perhaps. So much of her memory was gone. Her passage through Dream; the Night Train; the sky-vessel of Norrowa; the court of Nethermost London; the singing tiger; the travelling girl; all these things were like images from a half-remembered dream, falling away as she opened her eyes into a different reality.

'You must be the Hallowe'en King,' she said.

He turned to her and smiled. 'Must I? Then I suppose you must be right. Well met, Queen Orfeia,' he said, and held out his hand in greeting.

But Fay did not take it; instead she watched in horror as he faced her, the illusion of beauty falling from his person like a garment. For the Hallowe'en King was handsome only in profile: one side of his body was that of a well-proportioned, fine-looking man, the other was shrunken and skeletal; and the hand he held out to greet her was nothing but a handful of bones under the rings of silver. One eye was dark as honeycomb in the living part of his face; the other shone blue as glaciers in a socket of burnished bone. For Death has two faces; the face of memory and Dream, which endure in spite of everything, and that of darkness and despair. And now Fay remembered the tailor bee's words: *Take nothing, not even a handshake from him, for if you do, you and your Daisy will stay in his kingdom for ever.*

And so she smiled at the Hallowe'en King, and knelt to kiss the hem of his robe (making sure to keep to his living side), and said: 'I come not as a Queen, my Lord, but as a humble supplicant. You have my daughter Daisy. I am here to plead for her return, just as she was taken from me.'

The Hallowe'en King gave his tilted half-smile. 'It has been some time since Death surrendered one of its people. What do you have to offer me?'

'Anything you want,' said Fay.

The Hallowe'en King raised an eyebrow. 'And what *do* I want, my Queen?' he said. 'I have everything my heart could desire. My kingdom is a thousand times greater than any realm that has ever been. I have wealth beyond the dreams of any lord of the living. I can see into every World; every antechamber of Dream. Whatever you have will one day be mine: every thought; every memory. Knowing this, how can you hope to seduce me into doing your will?'

The King was right, thought Fay to herself. She had nothing to offer him. And yet, the King in Alberon's tale had managed to reach his cruel heart. She summoned a smile, although she felt very small, very wan in his presence. 'Music is my currency,' she said, remembering Alberon's tale. 'I can sing a song so gay that even the dust will stand up and dance. I can sing a song so true that even the dead will listen. Let me sing for you, my King, and if I can make you weep—'

'I have heard this claim before,' said the Hallowe'en King, with a smile. 'That tale has been told, and the riddle, too. Such child's play may have brought you here, but if you hope to win my favour, you cannot expect to do so with a tale that has been told a thousand times before.'

'Oh,' said Fay in a small voice.

The King went on, his golden eye shining with amusement. 'But yes, my Queen, I know of your voice. And I do *so* love a challenge.' He smiled again, and once more Fay saw both charm and horror in his smile. 'Very well. You may sing for me. But I too am accounted to have something of a musical flair. You shall match my voice with yours in contest, and we shall see whose is the most eloquent. We shall sing three times, my Queen, and if you win, you shall have your way. But if *I* win' – his blue eye glittered like ice – 'then you shall stay here, in my realm, and share my throne for ever.'

Fay took no time to consider it. 'Done,' she said, and

the Hallowe'en King put out his living hand to shake. 'Have no fear,' he said, seeing her pause. 'This is no trick. The ruler of the Land of Death can never break their word, for fear that all the Worlds be thrown into chaos and disarray.'

Fay took his hand (it was long and cool and pale, and laden with many silver rings). 'I agree to your bargain,' she said. 'If I win, my daughter goes back with me to the land of the living. If I lose, I stay here with you. Now let the contest begin.'

And at that, the King lifted his hand, and once more, the mournful scenery changed, and Fay found herself in a banqueting hall, filled with the trappings of the dead.

Four

At first glance, the banqueting hall was not unlike that of King Alberon. But where the court of London Beneath was lit with living torchflies, the cavernous hall of the Hallowe'en King was garlanded with foxfire. The ceiling was vaulted with fungi that shone with a ghostly greenish light, and the walls were alive with curlicues of bioluminescence. In its undersea light, she could see the bone-white throne of the Hallowe'en King, and among the pillars that lined the hall, she could see the ranks of the dead, standing there like an army of shadows. She could hear their voices, too: a kind of rushing, whispering sound, not unlike the sound of the sea. *All* sounds resemble the sound of the sea, when multiplied to infinity, and the gathered dead were like grains of sand endlessly shifting and moving, until the air was alive with the sound and the restlessness of their presence.

And now she could see that the hall was all bones: there were skulls lining the portals, and spines along the architraves, and set into the smooth pale polished floor was a mosaic of finger-bones. On the walls there were tapestries of rich and marvellous design, spun from the hair of a million dead, depicting scenes of dancing, and battle, and feasting and merrymaking. And, as in the court of King Alberon, there were tables laden with dainties from all the known Worlds: delicate fruits from Fiddler's Green; sea urchins from Atlantis, served on a bed of luminous seaweed; flower-wines from Tír na nÓg; spiced pastries from Antillia.

Fay was so hungry she felt almost faint. But even so, she knew not to touch of the food of the Land of Death. Not a drop of wine, not a seed could safely pass between her lips. She looked neither left nor right as she passed between the laden tables, moving towards the end of the banqueting hall. Behind her, she heard the sounds of the tables with their tempting wares crumbling back into the dust, but she did not spare them a second glance, nor did she stop until she was standing at the foot of the throne, where the Hallowe'en King awaited her, flanked by two of his servants.

These servants were colourful creatures of

indeterminate gender and race; one with extravagant purple hair, the other, in what seemed to be a mask adorned with blinking eyes. *I've seen them somewhere before*, thought Fay, but try as she might, she could not remember the circumstances of their meeting. The creature with the purple hair grinned, revealing a set of long, sharp teeth. The creature in the mask made a sound like someone scraping a violin, and Fay realized it wasn't a mask, but the nightmarish face of an insect.

'You mustn't mind Cobweb and Peronelle,' said the King with a lazy smile. 'But entertainments such as this are few in the Land of Shadows.'

He gestured languidly towards Fay. 'My Queen, I trust that this attire does justice to the occasion?'

Fay looked down at her clothing and saw that she was dressed in a beautiful gown of blue-green moiré, with gemstones clasped around her neck and cascading into her décolletage. The Hallowe'en King, too, had taken pains with his appearance. Gone was his skeletal aspect. His face was once more handsome beneath his crown of dead man's ivory; his form once more harmonious, his smile entirely charming. His cloak was made from ten thousand skins of the long-extinct Cloudrunner mink, and his boots were of dragonfly leather that reflected the undersea glow of the walls.

Fay met the Hallowe'en King's eyes: one honey-golden; the other, ice-blue. 'I prefer to keep my own clothes,' she said, remembering what the tailor bee had told her in the caverns.

He shrugged. 'Whatever my Queen desires.'

Fay found herself back in her hoodie, barefoot, her bare legs covered in scratches.

'Thank you,' said Fay. The Hallowe'en King seemed unmoved by the tartness in her voice. He smiled at her with deceptive charm, and with a wave of his pale hand, dismissed the scene around them. Gone now was the banqueting hall: instead, the hall of the Hallowe'en King had become a theatre, larger than any Fay had ever seen or imagined.

There were rows and rows of seats, reaching into the distance – stalls, dress circle, upper circles, many boxes and balconies – all upholstered in velvet as dark as blood, and gilded with the bioluminescence of the Underworld. Fay and the King were standing on the largest stage she had ever seen, with curtains that reached up to the ceiling vaults, and dizzying catwalks, and footlights like St Elmo's fire, and many elaborate carvings of angels and dragons and mythical beasts, all gleaming with the strange energies of the Kingdom of the Dead. The audience was the ranks of the dead, remade by the King from the dust of the past. All of them pale and attentive; all in their finest evening dress. Moth and Peronelle were there, too, in the front row of the stalls, whispering behind their fans of spider silk and filigreed bone. The gleam of gems; the rustle of silks; the breathless hush of an audience awaiting a much-anticipated performance – all this was so familiar, and yet so very strange, that Fay was suddenly sure that she had never left London Before, that she was asleep and dreaming.

The Hallowe'en King smiled again, and Fay saw that he was holding a gilded harp that shimmered in the footlights.

'This harp was made from the bones of a girl who died at the hands her lover,' he said. 'The strings were made from her golden hair, the crown from her skull, the pegs from her toes, the pedestal from her pelvis. It was fashioned by a craftsman long dead; a luthier whose name was once renowned across the Nine Worlds, and this instrument was the last of his work: the rest has long since gone into dust. What will serve to accompany *you*, my Queen, in our musical contest?'

Fay looked around. 'I—' she faltered.

The King's smile broadened. 'Brave of you to go unaccompanied,' he said. 'But I must trust that you are prepared.'

For a moment Fay was aware of her courage beginning to fail. But then she remembered the seashell in

the pouch of her hoodie, and felt its reassuring weight against her lower belly. She held it out to the Hallowe'en King and summoned her brightest, bravest smile.

'This will be my instrument,' she said with a confidence she did not feel. 'A conch from the shores of Norrowa, its music the voice of the ocean.'

The King's smile did not falter, but the fingers of his living hand tapped an impatient rhythm against his throne of dead man's ivory.

'Then, my Queen, let us begin,' he said in his smooth and gracious voice. With a languid gesture, the King summoned a bright, narrow spotlight, and Fay Orr lifted the shell to her lips and began to play for her daughter's life.

Five

The shell had sounded like whalesong to her on the beach of Norrowa. In the hall of the Hallowe'en King, it sounded still more melancholy, still more mysterious and strange, and it made her think of the Night Train's horn, as she heard it in Nethermost London. And, as its echo resonated across the auditorium, Fay raised her voice and started to sing a song from the days of her stage career.

It was the song of a woman who has given up everything she has; a song of broken dreams, lost hopes, and a mother's enduring love. It had been a long time since she had sung it, and she was out of practice, but her voice had its own kind of memory. It soared into the waiting air; it torched the theatre vaulting into frantic luminescence; it stirred the innumerable dead like a forest of fallen leaves. In the front row, Moth and Peronelle leaned forward in their seats, lips parted, eyes glittering. But Fay sang only to the King. Half-turned towards him on his throne, she looked straight into his face and sang; and saw the sum of all her grief reflected in his living eye.

At the end of the song, there was applause just like the sound of waves of a beach, and the Hallowe'en King gave Fay a tiny nod of appreciation.

'Brava, Queen Orfeia,' he said. 'Your voice is sweet as honeycomb. Now, my Queen, let us see what I can bring to this contest.' And, lifting the gilded harp, he ran his living hand across the strings, and a strange and beautiful music filled the theatre of the dead.

It was like no harp Fay had ever heard. It sounded like a human voice, sweet and sad and far away, and when the King's voice joined it, they made a single, perfect resonance. And the Hallowe'en King sang a song of love; of longing and of sorrow. It was a song about letting go of all the joys and dreams of Life; of sleeping next to a lover, a child, and knowing that happiness cannot last. The voice of the King was more resonant than any Fay had ever known; its tenderness was astonishing, its compassion endless. And at the end, the applause was like the raging of a storm, and

Fay found herself almost in tears, and knew that he had won the round.

'Now for your second song, my Queen,' said the Hallowe'en King with a smile. 'I'm sure you must have many more in your extensive repertoire.'

Fay did not answer, but looked at the boards as the spotlight moved back onto her. She could see that, in spite of the glare, her shadow was barely visible. And now, as she tried to think of a song, she realized that her memory, so rich with music a moment before, had vanished like a handful of dust. Not a lyric, not a tune could she recall from her West End days. The part of her that had trodden the boards, that had recorded albums, that had sung duets with Allan, that had picked up flowers on the stage and hung up costumes in dressing-rooms – all of that was gone for ever. Her career had been erased in the time it took her to sing one solo.

And now she had to do it again: and what might it cost her this time? Fay was aware she had already lost a significant part of her memory. Only a handful of fragments remained of her life in London Before, and yet, while there was breath in her, she would fight for Daisy's life; and Death himself would not stop her.

And so she raised the shell to her lips and summoned the sound of the Night Train's horn: then she

sang to the Hallowe'en King the only scrap of melody
that she could still remember:

> *My plaid away, my plaid away,*
> *My plaid shall not be blown away.*

The simple tune sounded out of place and strange
in the cavernous theatre. Fay found herself very conscious of her bare legs under the hoodie; of grubby
hands and her tangled hair; of the faces of the dead
watching her, reflections in a mirror maze—

What am I doing here? she thought, and for a terrible
moment she could not recall who she was, or why she
was standing there in the spotlight. Looking down at
the boards, she saw that she cast almost no shadow.
Am I even here at all? And why is someone clapping?

She turned to see the Hallowe'en King, applaud-
ing her with a twisted smile. 'A brave attempt, Queen
Orfeia,' he said. He had once more assumed his true
aspect, and his dead eye shone like polished chrome
as he picked up his instrument.

'Your voice is sweet as ever,' he said, 'although
your material lacks in range.' And then he touched the
strings of his harp with the skeletal fingers of his dead
hand, and the theatre of the dead was filled with a terrible music. And the Hallowe'en King sang a song of

pain, of sacrifice and suffering. His blue eye shone like starlight, and his voice was rich as blood. He sang of great loves gone to dust; of empires built and fallen; of long-abandoned philosophies and of gods reduced to children's toys. And Fay looked up at the bone-white throne and knew that the King had won the round, and that Daisy was lost to her, for ever, and without recall.

Six

The applause for the King's performance went on for a long time. It could have continued for ever, had not the King dismissed it with a wave of his skeletal hand. At the gesture, his audience of the dead, in all their gems and finery, vanished back into the dust, and the great auditorium was left empty and echoing. Except for Moth and Peronelle, still standing by the front of the stage; their finery gone, their gowns transformed into scant and colourless rags.

'I think we can do without them, don't you?' said the Hallowe'en King, and, with a gesture, he banished the pair. Then, turning again to Fay, he smiled; and although his smile was unbearable, she thought she saw in his one living eye something like compassion. 'You fought a brave battle, my Queen,' he said, 'but

Death always wins. You must know that.' Still smiling, he held out his skeletal hand. 'Come to me, Queen Orfeia, and you will learn that I can be kind. My kingdom has no limits. It can be anything you want it to be. Do you wish for company? I can give you handmaidens, entertainers, dancers, clowns. I can make the halls of Death ring with music and laughter. Are you hungry? I can bring you wines and fruits from every World. I can build you a library of a hundred thousand books; I can give you gardens filled with the most fragrant of flowers. Only stay, and rule at my side, and I will give you your heart's desire.'

Fay looked for her shadow on the boards. For a moment she thought it had disappeared. But then she saw it – the tiniest, the most translucent shimmering, less than a heat-haze, less than the glimpse of a moth's wing through gossamer – and knew that her task was incomplete. She still had *something* to bring to the fight, though what that was, she did not know. Playing for time, she looked up at the King, and said:

'You promised three rounds.'

'But I have already won,' said the King. 'What purpose would a third round serve? Already, your shadow is well nigh gone, and with it, much of your memory. Stop now, and join me, and keep the memory of your Daisy. If it amuses you, I can even bring her, sometimes, to keep you company.'

For a moment, Fay felt herself weaken. What was she still trying to prove? The King was much more powerful. Another attempt to match him would rob her of what little was left. There could be no shame in accepting defeat: after all, had not Mabs told her to keep her plaid, and her memories, close?

The Hallowe'en King seemed to guess her thoughts. 'Come to me,' he repeated, now holding out his living hand. 'Come to me. Take my hand, and you can see your Daisy.'

And with a gesture, he banished the lavish auditorium, with its empty seats and stifling draperies. In its place was a forest scene, with sunlight filtering through the leaves. It must have been spring, because Fay could see hawthorns in bloom, and the spikes of wild garlic, and primroses, and bluebells.

It was the scene she had glimpsed through the cracks in the pavement on Piccadilly. She felt a surge of fierce joy. It was real; so real that she could hear the leaves, smell the bluebells. And there was Daisy, lying asleep under a blanket embroidered with stars.

Instinctively, Fay started towards her. But even as her feet touched the grass, the idyllic scene faded away and she was alone with the Hallowe'en King in the dusty hall of the dead.

'The choice is yours,' said the Hallowe'en King. 'Your daughter by your side, or the loss of everything you have ever loved. Which is it to be, my Queen? Your King awaits your pleasure.'

Fay sighed and turned to face him again. The fleeting scent of bluebells still lingered in the dusty air. But it was an illusion, she knew, like all his other illusions. Nothing grew in the Kingdom of Death. Nothing was scented or beautiful.

The Hallowe'en King was still waiting, his living hand outstretched. She looked into his dead blue eye and said: 'Then hear my decision. If I must I will give myself to you, shadow and substance, body and soul. But we shall have our final round, whatever it may cost me.'

The Hallowe'en King shrugged. 'So be it,' he said. With a weary gesture, he summoned the stage and the spotlight. Fay could just see her shadow, pale as a petal on the boards. *Let the wind blow*, she thought. *Let the horn play. Whatever else you take from me, my plaid shall not be blown away.*

There was no auditorium now. But she needed a song. What was left to her but scraps? She reached into her pocket and drew out the tiny notebook.

Concealing it in the palm of her hand, she looked up at the Hallowe'en King and, summoning her most artless smile, said: 'May I make a request, my King? I need some time to collect my thoughts. Perhaps, if you were to perform first?'

The King raised an eyebrow. 'Playing for time? My Queen, we have all the time in the Worlds.' And he picked up his harp and ran his hands along the strings of golden hair that had been cut from a murdered girl, long ago and far away.

'I wonder,' said Fay, 'could I make a request for the ballad of King Orfeo? For I have heard only part of the tale, and long to know the whole story.'

The Hallowe'en King gave a tiny frown over his gilded harp of bone. 'The ballad of King Orfeo?' he said. 'What makes you speak of that old tale?'

Fay said: 'I heard it in London Beneath. A pretty tale, with a haunting melody. But I never heard how it ended. And so, if it please Your Majesty, I would have you tell me how King Orfeo lost his shadow.'

The Hallowe'en King seemed to hesitate. Then he shrugged his shoulders and said: 'If that is your wish, so be it, my Queen.' And he started to tell her the story.

The Shadowless Man

≈

'Yees tak your lady, an yees gaeng hame,
An yees be king ower a' your ain.'
He's taen his lady, an he's gaen hame,
An noo he's king ower a' his ain.

Child Ballad no. 19: *King Orfeo*

One

'Long ago,' began the King, 'long ago and far away, when all the Worlds were honeycomb, King Orfeo went to the Land of the Dead to plead for the return of his Queen. The Hallowe'en King was moved by his song, and agreed to release the lady, but Death is one of the Trickster's line, and his gift was a cruel one.

'Returning home to his own land, King Orfeo found his wife much changed. Her time in the Kingdom of Death had made her cold and unresponsive. And then one day, Orfeo awoke to find that she had fled his side, forsaking her realm and her subjects, and leaving no clue to her whereabouts. For six long years, King Orfeo sought her all across the Worlds, but when he found her, he realized that she no longer knew him. She had fallen in love with a commoner, and given him a daughter, whom she loved more than anything. She remembered nothing of her life, her encounter with Death, or even her name.

'And yet the King would not let go – *could* not let go – of his love for her. He went to consult the Oracle, to find out how to win her back, but the Oracle merely responded with mockery and riddles. And so the King took his golden harp and journeyed back to the Land of the Dead. The road was long and dangerous, but finally he reached Death's shore, and called for its ruler to come to him.

'"You lied to me, Lord Death," he cried. "You promised to return my wife. But the woman I brought home with me is *not* my wife. You kept back her shadow, and with it, her memory of the love she once bore me. Thus, by the bond Death cannot break, I challenge you to face me."

'The Lord of the Kingdom of Death took his time in answering the summons. When he finally appeared, regal in his hawkmoth cloak and his crown of dead man's ivory, his face was grim, and his living eye gleamed with a fearsome anger.

'"You called me a liar," he said; and although his voice was very soft, the Nine Worlds shivered at the sound. "No one in the Nine Worlds has ever called me a liar."

'"Then seek satisfaction," said Orfeo, "and we shall see whose cause is just."

'Lord Death gave a crack of laughter. "You think you can win against me? I am Death. By my nature, I win *all* battles."

'"Then you cannot fail to win this one," said King Orfeo, smiling.

'Lord Death gave his twisted smile, although deep down he was puzzled. What could King Orfeo hope to achieve through a duel? How could a mortal defeat Death?

'"Very well," he said at last. "Name your weapon."

'"I have it here," said Orfeo, holding out his golden harp. "I challenge you to a contest for my lady's shadow. The one who wins will claim her heart, and take her, either to the Land of Death, or back to the land of the Living."

'The Ruler of the Land of Death considered the words of King Orfeo. "Very well," he said at last. "But if you lose, I will take you both, body and soul, for ever."

'King Orfeo smiled. "Agreed," he said. "But you are ruler of this land. Everything in it obeys you. I request the right to hold our contest in neutral territory. Let us hold it in Dream, where neither of us has the advantage."

'Lord Death frowned at King Orfeo's words. "Death cannot leave his realm," he said, "without risking disaster."

'"But time has no meaning in Dream," said the King. "In Dream, a lifetime may pass, or a world can be built in a second. Our contest would pass in the blink of an eye. No one need even know of it."

'Lord Death considered the request. "Very well," he said at last. "We shall duel as you say."

'King Orfeo smiled. "I have but one more request."

'The Ruler of the Land of Death was surprised into laughter, for the first time in many years. He said: "Is there no end to your demands?" but his living eye shone with amusement.

'"Your living eye sees the Nine Worlds," King Orfeo went on humbly. "But your dead eye sees all that happens in Dream. To ensure that our duel is conducted in complete fairness, I would ask you to put it aside. Leave it here in Death, my Lord, and meet me, man to man, in Dream."

'Lord Death was of the Trickster's line, which meant he was suspicious. But it also meant he was arrogant. He knew that King Orfeo was the greatest musician alive, but Death is the master of everything and everyone that has ever lived, and he knew Orfeo could not win. And so he took out his all-seeing Eye and laid it on his bone-white throne, and Lord Death and King Orfeo stepped into Dream together.

'Death went first, and played a music so sublime that dreamers all across the Nine Worlds heard it, and wept, and smiled. Estranged lovers remembered their love and reached for each other in the dark; children called out for their mothers; old folk dreamed of summers past. King Orfeo heard it, and he knew that this was a contest he could not win.

'But the Trickster's line is a long one. King Orfeo, too, was a trickster, and he had taken years to make his plans. As Death played his melody in Dream, having left behind his all-seeing Eye, King Orfeo began to put his long-dreamed plan into action. The Oracle's riddles had proved easy to solve. The first answer was bees, the weavers of dream. The second, the land of Dream itself. And the third was Death, the shadowless land where the people themselves are all shadows.

'Now, he knew he must act fast. Time might *seem* endless in Dream, but in fact he had only seconds. First, he reached out to a dreamer, and sent her a vision of himself: a vision that would stay with her for all the years of her young life. Then, in an instant, he crossed into Death, and stood before the empty throne. And there he thought of the Oracle's words:

201

When you can walk shadowless at noon
Every sage grows merry in time
Hand in hand, once more you may
Lovers be; together again.

'For *this*, of course, had been the truth of the Oracle's prophecy. The only way for King Orfeo to be reunited with his beloved was to take the throne of the Hallowe'en King, and to assume his regency. And so he plucked out his left eye, and in its place put the Eye of the King, and sat himself on the bone-white throne, and put on the crown of ivory. And there he waited for many long years, knowing one day his lady would come; awaiting his chance to reclaim her.

'As for Lord Death – without his powers, he was left floating helpless in Dream, trapped in a web of music. Dream took his mind, but his music remained, spinning out into the Worlds like shining strands of spider silk. And there he remains eternally, for Hallowe'en Kings and Queens come and go, but Death is an ocean without any shore, and it endures for ever.'

The Hallowe'en King paused in his tale, and turned his mismatched eyes towards Fay. 'Are you sure you want the end of this tale?' he said, and his voice was gentle.

Fay nodded. 'Did she come?' she said. 'Did she answer his call from Dream?'

'Oh, his call was not to *her*,' said the Hallowe'en King with a smile. 'I told you, the Queen had already moved on. She had another family now; a daughter she loved more than Life itself. No, King Orfeo knew she would never respond to his voice. And so he called to someone else: his Queen's six-year-old daughter.'

Two

For a long time Fay said nothing. Her thoughts were like a tangle of briars; her heart like the Night Train's engine. It was all beginning to make sense to her, with the twisted logic of certain dreams: the Shadowless Man; the riddles; the rose – even her failing memory.

'You knew that if you took Daisy, I'd come,' she said at last, in a trembling voice. 'And you knew that bringing me here, like this, was the one sure way to make me forget her.'

The Hallowe'en King gave his twisted smile. 'Believe me, it hasn't been easy,' he said. 'I wasn't sure you'd make it this far. And yet you did. Your love brought you here. You followed the trail I left for you, all the way across the Worlds. I was in your daughter's dreams; I showed her to you in London Before. I led you closer, step by step, through the realm of Faërie, over the sea to Norrowa, into the maelstrom of Dream and finally, to the Shadowless Land. Through my all-seeing Eye I watched; and through your dreams I led you home.'

Fay listened to the Hallowe'en King, suddenly feeling very calm. There was a rushing sound in her head like that of a cold wind through the eaves. '*You* were King Orfeo,' she said. 'You were Daisy's Shadowless Man. *You're* the reason...' she went on, feeling the words turn to ice on her tongue. 'You're the reason she killed herself.'

He nodded. 'It was the only way. I did it because I love you, my Queen. Love greater than Life and stronger than Death. I did it all for you, for the sake of the love we had together.'

Fay felt the rushing sound in her head swell to a blizzard. 'And Alberon?' she said at last. 'Was he another illusion?'

'Do not despise illusions,' said the Hallowe'en King in his quiet voice. 'Glamours are how we show the truth that cannot be spoken. You loved me once, as Alberon, back in our realm of Faërie. I hoped you might remember me if I showed you what you had lost.'

Fay looked at him, and did not flinch at the sight of

his skeletal profile. 'I see,' she said. 'So what happens now?'

The Hallowe'en King raised his skeletal hand, and from the hall of dust there came a woman, all in white brocade. Her hair was longer than Fay's, and yet Fay still recognized her face – after all, she'd seen it in the mirror every day for the past forty years. But it was Fay as she *might* have been, in some alternate story: a fairy tale; a distant dream, from when the Worlds were honeycomb.

'Make a choice,' said the Hallowe'en King. 'Take my hand and you can reclaim your shadow; your true memories. You can be the woman you were; the woman with whom I fell in love. Your life among the Folk will be a fading dream, a candle flame that flickers out, leaving nothing but smoke behind.'

'And if I don't?' said Fay.

'Then you will be nothing; shadowless. It will be as if you never lived.'

Fay nodded slowly. 'And Daisy?'

'Forget her,' said the Hallowe'en King. 'You have *already* forgotten her. Take back your shadow and share my throne, and you shall be my Hallowe'en Queen, just as the Oracle prophesied.'

Fay looked at the shadow of herself standing before the bone-white throne. The other Fay was so beautiful

that she could hardly look at her, and yet she knew they were one and the same; reflections in a dark glass. For a moment, she found herself thinking of the statue over the Shaftesbury fountain: the one that so many call Eros.

Eros, god of love, she thought. So many cruel and selfish things have been done in Eros's name. Like the man before her now, who had lured an innocent girl to her death in order to satisfy his desire. Strange, that *he* should be revered, and his twin almost forgotten. And yet, that was *his* statue: Anteros, the selfless one; high against the London sky on wings as light as a butterfly's.

'Why do you hesitate?' said the King. 'I'm offering you eternal love. I am restoring you to your *real* life, to the future that was taken from us. Take back your shadow, and come to me, and we shall set the Worlds aflame. All you have to do is choose.'

And just for a moment, Fay could see the attraction of that future. Herself, immortal; perfected; all sorrow put away for good. Smiling, she reached out her hand—

And said: 'I'll take my turn now.'

Three

The Hallowe'en King made no protest, but Fay could sense his baffled rage. With a gesture, he banished the hall, the throne, and Fay found herself in a desert, bleak; unbroken to every horizon.

He faced her, one eye like a blade, the other dark with anger. 'Then take your turn, my Queen,' he said. 'And weep for what you could have had.'

Fay reached into her pocket for the shell, and into her memory for a song. Neither was forthcoming. She must have dropped the shell, she thought, while the King was telling his tale. And now, without a song to sing, she had no chance of matching him.

I had no chance anyway, she told herself. *And yet my Daisy shall have her song. If it costs me the very last drop of my blood: if it costs me my mind, she shall have it.*

And she opened the tiny notebook that she had kept in her pocket, and started to read in a low, clear voice, while all the time watching the thin heat-haze of her shadow on the ground. As she read the words aloud, they faded from the page like smoke, leaving the paper blank once more.

'The cake I made when she was four, shaped like Thomas the Tank Engine. The first time she went to the theatre.'

The Hallowe'en King narrowed his living eye. 'This is pointless, my Lady,' he said. 'I beg you, spare us both this charade.'

Fay ignored him and went on. 'The sandcastle we built, on the beach in Brighton. In the coffee shop at King's Cross, with a cup of chocolate. Feeding the squirrels in Green Park.'

'Please, my Lady,' said the King, and she thought his voice was unsteady. 'Let us have no more of this.'

Fay went on ignoring him. Her voice rang out across the sand. 'Her first day at school. Her first Christmas. Her midnight-blue tent, embroidered with stars. In the park on Bonfire Night, writing our names with a sparkler. Grabbing my finger, the day she was born. It felt as if she would never let go.'

'Don't,' said the King in an urgent voice. 'Just take my hand, and I'll release her. Only stop this madness.

Take my hand, and I promise you—'

'Her name was Daisy. Her favourite toy—'

The King made a sound of anger and pain, and Fay saw tears in his living eye.

'—her favourite toy was a tiger.'

She looked down at the hot pale sand, searching for her shadow. But looking down, she found it gone, and now she realized that she could no longer remember the toy, or even the colour of Daisy's eyes.

Then she looked back at the notebook, and saw that all the pages were blank.

Four

Time passes differently in Death, if it can be said to pass at all. Fay had no sense of how long it was before she looked back at the Hallowe'en King. He was watching her with a strange expression, and Fay saw that his eyes were wet. His features, too, looked different to her: and she thought the dead side of his face looked no longer hideous, but simply exhausted and very sad.

A gesture of his living hand summoned the woodland scene again, but this time Fay could feel the grass under her feet, and the bluebells gave off a wistful scent. Daisy's eyes were opening, drowsily, as if from a dream.

Blue. Her eyes are blue, thought Fay. *Her eyes are blue, and I love her.*

She glanced back at the Hallowe'en King. 'I don't understand. What's happening?'

'I have released your Daisy,' he said. 'The Night Train will take her back to her World, to a time before her accident. She will have no memory of this place, or the Shadowless Man. Her mind will be healed of its trouble, and she will live a long and happy life.'

Fay stared at him. 'I don't understand.'

'You won the contest,' said the King. 'The Lord of Death concedes defeat.'

213

'But how?' said Fay.

He gave a slow, unhappy smile. 'I loved you, my Queen,' he told her, 'with all the passion of Eros. But yours was the love of Anteros, the love that makes not a single demand, but gives, and gives, and gives, no matter what it loses. And that I cannot equal, not in this, or any World.'

Fay nodded. 'Thank you.'

'As for you, shadowless as you are, I cannot restore your memory. If I could, I would, but that gift is beyond the power of Death. But if you choose, you are free to return once more to the World of the living. I will not stand in your way, or pursue you any longer.'

Fay closed her eyes and breathed in the lovely scent of the bluebells. It felt as if she were breathing it in for the very first time; the new grass at her feet was soft; the air was bright as butterflies. A marvellous emptiness filled her mind; and with it a deep contentment, as if she had accomplished some gruelling task that she could no longer remember; and with it, a love as vast as the sky; as wide and deep as the ocean.

Blue. Her eyes are blue, she thought.

'Goodbye. I love you, Daisy.'

And then she smiled at the Hallowe'en King, and reached out to clasp his skeletal hand …

The Hallowe'en Queen

≈

One

They say that the madcap Queen of the Fae once fell in love with a child of the Folk, and brought her back from the Shadowless Land, forsaking her life and her memory.

And sometimes, in her dreams, she caught a fleeting glimpse of what she had lost, and heard the music of days gone by, and awoke with tears in her living eye. And sometimes in her dreams, she ran, endlessly, through London streets, and heard the voice of another woman, calling her from between the Worlds, and *almost* remembered what she had known, long ago and far away. But still she was content with her choice, for in dreams she remembered her daughter.

Almost every fairy tale begins with the death of the parents. That is how it is meant to be. That is how it has always been. But Death is not the end of the tale; merely another verse of a song. And love is a bird that never dies, but soars through the sky, and sings the song it cannot keep from singing.

For a song can climb higher, live longer, see more than any bird that ever flew. A song can pass from mouth to mouth, changing with the seasons. A song can pass between the Worlds, even to the Kingdom of Death, where the Hallowe'en Queen on her bone-white throne watches the Worlds through her all-seeing Eye, and contemplates the honeycomb.

This is the story of such a song. A song born of a mother's love, given wings by a mother's grief. A song of memory, and loss, and of the magic of every-day things. A song of rebirth, and rejoicing; the song of a journey to Death and beyond. And its variations are endless, and the song is never over.